Only Ever Neighbors

Only Ever Neighbors

SHAELA KAY

Blue Water Books
Richland, WA

*For my dear friend Carrie "Cordy" Jensen,
whose knowledge, expertise, and encouragement have
been invaluable to this story*

Chapter 1

My life has always had a plan. An organized, check-the-box, follow-the-rules kind of plan. And since I was a freshman in high school, the plan consisted of getting into design school, graduating with honors, and working my way up through the hierarchy of fashion to become one of the top designers in the country. I dream of seeing my designs on runways and red carpets across the world. From L.A. to New York and Paris to Beijing, the name *Taylor O'Neill* will someday be on the lips of everyone worth knowing. I'll be famous, and my designs will be sought after far and wide.

Yep, that's the plan. Go big or go home, right?

Right. So when my cute neighbor, Logan, asks me to dinner as I'm leaving for work, I don't even hesitate.

"I wish I could," I say, locking the door to my apartment, "but I've got a deadline to meet so I'll probably be working late."

"Always working," he says with a half-hearted grin.

I smile back. "Yep. Groceries don't buy themselves, you know." I give a small wave and head down the stairs.

"How about tomorrow night?" he calls.

"See ya!" I say, rushing out of the building.

It's not that I don't like the guy. He's polite and kind of cute, in a Clark Kent-meets-Peter Parker kind of way. And as far as I can tell, he's close to my own twenty-six years. But as I mentioned before, I have a very detailed plan to reach my goals, and nowhere on my spreadsheet is there room for a relationship.

Well. Maybe in cell 72C. But I'd better not risk it.

I take the subway to work, hardly noticing the foot traffic I pass on the way to the station. Life in New York City is far less glamorous than all the movies I watched growing up made it out to be. More crowded, too. But I love it here, and since NYC is the fashion hub for the Western Hemisphere, I'd never want to live anywhere else.

I get off at Penn Station and head down 7th. Totsworth & Company has their headquarters on the fourth floor of a generic office building a couple blocks away. Even though designing children's clothing isn't exactly *haute couture,* it pays the bills, and it's better than designing men's underwear (don't ask me how I know this).

"'Morning, Sam," I say, sweeping past the receptionist on the way to my cubicle. She's on a call and doesn't even acknowledge me, which is fine, since I have a million things to do to get ready for my presentation this afternoon.

Working in the fashion industry means I often have the odd sensation that I'm living in a time warp: the current time, which is early spring in New York, and work time, which is currently midwinter. But that's the nature of fashion—we have to stay at least two seasons ahead if we want production to stay on schedule. Even though it's only March, we've been prepping for our Christmas collection for weeks already, and today is the big reveal. My boss, Greg, likely expected me to design another cozy, traditional collection, but I've got other plans.

I work through lunch, putting the finishing touches to my presentation and making sure all the fabric samples are pressed and ready to go. The staff meeting is at three o'clock, which makes the afternoon drag and my stomach revolt. It's a good thing I skipped lunch because I probably wouldn't have been able to keep anything down. Nerves always make me nauseous.

At two forty-five I head to the conference room with my stack of folders and fabric, anxious and excited. This is only my second time heading up a full collection, and the others will probably think I'm crazy for breaking tradition and trying something new. But Greg liked my new ideas for the summer collection last year, and I'm willing to take the risk.

I put my laptop and fabric swatches on the table, then walk around placing a slim black folder in front of each chair. A couple seats are already occupied, and my coworker Phil starts flipping through the file as soon as I set it in front of him.

"Getting bold, eh Taylor?" he says with a cheeky grin. I smile, but my stomach quivers.

"Just keeping things fresh," I reply, taking my seat. I open my laptop, but notice Phil make a face and shake his head at Jennifer a few seats down.

I clench my teeth. Who cares what they think? All that matters is whether or not I can sell the idea and my designs to Greg, because he has the final say. If Greg approves the collection, the others will have to jump on board to see it come to fruition, or risk losing their jobs. *I just need to impress Greg.*

The rest of the department files in over the next few minutes, chatting about various projects or things going on in their personal lives. I keep my eyes trained on my keyboard, trying to stay focused.

"Alright everyone, let's get this meeting started," Greg calls, taking his seat. "I promised my wife I'd be home for dinner so this can't go any longer than an hour."

I sit up a bit straighter in my seat, my nerves buzzing like I've had one too many lattes. The chatter around the table dies down, and all eyes focus on our boss.

"As you all know," Greg says, "I've asked Taylor to head up our Christmas collection this year. She did a phenomenal job on summer last year and I'm sure we won't be disappointed with her ideas for the holidays. Taylor, tell us what you've got."

I get to my feet and move to the head of the table. "Thanks Greg," I say, willing my voice not to tremble. "I was thrilled to be asked to design such an iconic collection for Totsworth & Company, and I hope my designs will excite and inspire you."

Around the table, my coworkers open their folders and begin flipping through the pages. I see a few raised brows and hear a couple murmurs, but I set my jaw and forge ahead.

"As you can see, I've decided to break from the traditional red and green color palette we see so often for this time of year. My collection is entitled 'Winter Wonderland' and will showcase clothing and accessories in various hues of icy blue and royal purple, with silver and iridescent accent colors and accessories."

The murmurs grow, and I chance a glance at Greg's face. He isn't smiling.

"But isn't this supposed to be a *Christmas* collection?"

The question comes from Jan, who's been with the company longer than I've been alive. I smile tightly.

"It *is* a Christmas collection, but it goes beyond that.

Christmas has quite a limited shelf life. Customers purchase holiday wear for only about six weeks leading up to Christmas, but there's a huge drop off in January. I thought we could capitalize on the winter season as a whole rather than just the festivities in December."

Jan frowns, flipping through the pages again. The man sitting next to her clears his throat.

"It's certainly not the usual," he says, almost hesitant to share his opinion, "but I find it refreshing. Red and green are Christmas colors, but there are other holidays besides Christmas in December. Hanukkah and Kwanzaa, for instance."

"Yes, exactly," I say, grateful for the boost. "A winter collection is far more inclusive than simply a Christmas one."

The meeting continues. I take everyone through the signature pieces and the materials I've chosen, passing around the samples I've brought with me. I field questions and try to stop myself from glancing too often at Greg's face, but I can't help it. I'm not sure if what I see there is encouraging or not.

The meeting lasts just under an hour. I answer a few last minute questions before Greg finally clears his throat, the signal to everyone that we need to wrap things up. I take my seat again, smiling in gratitude at the few coworkers who showed enthusiasm for my designs, and watching the others— the majority—avoid my eyes.

My heart sinks.

"Thank you, Taylor," Greg says, getting to his feet. "You've certainly put a lot of thought into this and your presentation was very impressive. I have a few questions for you, but we can handle those privately. See you all tomorrow."

The room hums with the sound of many voices as I gather

my things and head back to my desk. Greg catches up to me before I can even set it all down.

"Taylor, come see me in my office, please."

He's already walking away by the time I look up, which isn't a good sign. I sigh, dreading what I know is coming.

"Have a seat," he says when I step inside the room. I shut the door and take the chair in front of his desk.

"Good job on the presentation today," he says. "You have a great eye for color and your collection is certainly unique."

I raise one eyebrow at him. "But?"

He sighs. "But I don't think we're going to be able to use your designs. They're just... not what our customers expect from us."

"But what about the consumers who aren't our customers yet? Maybe this is what will get them to purchase our clothing and try our brand."

Greg opens his mouth to say something, but I press on.

"I don't think we're going to lose any of our loyal customers," I say. "If anything, it will shake things up with them. Maybe they're tired of seeing the same things, year after year. This is something new, something they will want *because* it's new."

"Taylor, I appreciate your enthusiasm, I really do," he says, "but it's just not a risk I'm prepared to take. If you had designed a collection that was more traditional, with a bit of blue and silver thrown in, well then, that would probably have gone over well. Tested the waters, see, to gauge our customer's interest."

I sit back, deflated.

"It's nothing personal, Taylor, you know that," he says more gently. "It's business. Business is all about taking calculated risks, and weighing the pros and cons of making changes. More than eighty percent of our December revenue comes from our Christmas collection each year, and that's too much to risk losing for something so drastically different."

I hear his words and nod, but inside I'm screaming. Four years at one of the top design schools in the nation, and for what? To have my vision and talent tossed out the window for the sake of tradition?

"Look, I know you're disappointed," Greg says. "If you'd like to try again, I'll need a new portfolio by the end of next week. Or I can ask Marjorie and Jason to draw up a new collection based on a previous year's designs."

Marjorie and Jason, the Totsworth dream team. They've designed and released more collections than any other designer or duo, and I was ecstatic to be chosen over them, especially after only three years with the company. There's no way I'm giving *that* up as well.

"No, I can manage," I say. "I'll have another portfolio on your desk next week."

The office is mostly empty by the time I collect my things and head for the train. My brain is in a disappointed fog, and it's a miracle I get off at the right stop. I trudge up the stairs to my apartment, the door across the landing opening as I pull out my keys.

"Hey, Taylor," I hear in Logan's cheerful voice. "I thought you were working late?"

I turn to see my neighbor holding a trash bag, obviously on his way to the dumpster.

"Change of plans," I say. "My work schedule was interrupted by a date with a glass of wine and Netflix."

"Oh. Rough day?"

"Yeah."

"Sorry." He looks like he might want to say more, but instead he indicates the bag in his hand. "I, uh, better get this thrown out. See ya."

"See ya."

I step inside my apartment and kick off my shoes. Walking into the living room, I slump down on the couch and lay my head back, closing my eyes.

A few minutes later there's a light knock on the door. Considering the fact that I haven't yet ordered dinner and it's too late for any packages to arrive, I have a good idea who it might be.

"Hey, Logan," I say, trying not to sigh as I open the door.

"Hey," he says, looking self-conscious. He pushes his glasses up the bridge of his nose. "I'm sorry that you had a bad day."

I shrug. "It happens."

"Do you, uh... do you want to talk about it?"

His voice is hesitant, as if he's worried he might be overstepping his bounds.

I smile ruefully. "If this is your way of asking me out again after what I said this morning, I'm really not in the mood."

His face immediately turns red. "No, it's not that, I just... I mean..." He blows out his breath in a shaky laugh. "Sorry. That's not what I was trying to do, I just... thought you could use a friend," he finishes with a lift of his shoulder.

I study him for a minute. His hair is neither blond nor brown, but that mousey color in between the two, and it looks coarse and wiry, sticking out in odd directions. He moved into the building a few months ago and I don't know much about him, but my gut tells me he's harmless.

"I don't have many friends," I murmur, almost to myself. "Too busy chasing my dreams. Sticking to the plan."

"Everyone needs a friend sometimes," he says quietly.

We lapse into silence, but after a moment I sigh and step back, jerking my head toward the living room. "Do you want a glass of wine?"

His face flames again. "Oh. Um, thanks, but I don't drink."

"Oh." I blink. "Really?" I blurt, before I can stop myself.

He clears his throat. "Yeah. But I appreciate the offer. Do you... I mean, would you like to grab a coffee instead?"

He looks adorably uncomfortable, with his glasses sliding down his nose and his hair sticking out in haphazard spikes. I can't help the smile that tugs at my lips. "Sure. Coffee would be great. Let me put my things away and I'll be out in ten minutes."

Chapter 2

The last time I went on a first date I vowed never to trust dating apps again, because the man I was *supposed* to meet for drinks had a profile picture indicating that he had hair, teeth, and was somewhere between the ages of twenty and forty. The man I ACTUALLY met had about as much hair as a naked mole rat, and the same two front teeth. He was also old enough to be my grandfather, which made the awkward encounter a little too creepy. He didn't seem at all surprised by my appearance, since apparently I missed the memo about not being truthful in my profile and photo. Needless to say, I had a quick drink with Gramps, excused myself to the ladies room, and high-tailed it out the back door. I sent him a message through the app (thank goodness I hadn't given him my personal number) and immediately deleted my profile.

There's a first and last time for everything, I guess.

Even though I wouldn't classify getting coffee with my neighbor as a *date*, it has the same feel as a first date, since we don't know each other all that well. We make idle chitchat as we walk down the street to our local caffeine dealer, talking about the mundane things no one really cares about. We order our drinks and find a cozy little table in the corner by the front window, and as I shrug out of my jacket Logan pulls my chair out for me. I stare at him.

"Um. That's very... chivalrous of you," I say, giving him an awkward, questioning smile.

He shrugs, slightly pink. "Habit. My mom taught me young."

The man learned chivalry from his mother? Huh. Maybe he's from the South?

"So. Tell me about your day," he says, taking the seat across from me.

"Wow. Did your mother teach you subtlety, too? Or are you a psychologist?"

His flush deepens, and I realize he doesn't know me well enough yet to understand my humor.

"I'm kidding," I say. "It's fine." Then I lift my shoulder in a shrug. "There's not much to tell. My boss didn't like my proposal during a meeting today and wants me to start over at square one." I shake my head. "All that work," I murmur, more to myself than to him.

"Yikes. I'm sorry to hear that. Was it a big project?"

I nod as the barista comes over with our drinks. "Yeah. I've been working on it for weeks. And I *nailed* my presentation today, it just..." I sigh. "It just wasn't what he wanted."

We sip our drinks—decaf cappuccino for me, Earl Gray tea for him—in silence for a few moments.

"You're a fashion designer, right?" he asks.

I nod. "For Totsworth and Company."

"Kids' clothes?"

11

I raise an eyebrow at him over my mug. "You sound surprised."

"I am," he says. "I mean, I'm sure you're great and all, but I guess I always pictured you as the next Coco Chanel or whatever. Runway models and all that."

I blink. "You did?"

"Yeah." He sits up, looking a bit more animated. "You have that air about you, you know? I mean, I don't really know that fashion designers have a specific persona," he gestures haphazardly in my general direction, "but you always look amazing and—" He chokes on a cough, probably realizing how that sounds, "and, um, I guess that's how I picture them." He buries his face in his cup, his ears a bright shade of pink.

If anyone else had said that to me, I'd have rolled my eyes and quipped something about them not being much of a fisherman. But coming from my socially-awkward-yet-surprisingly-sweet neighbor makes it endearing. His obvious embarrassment at the accidental compliment makes it all the more adorable.

I smile at him as he struggles to regain his composure. "Thanks," I say, taking a sip from my own cup.

After a minute he clears his throat. "Sorry about that. I'm not really good with this kind of thing."

"What kind of thing?"

He looks down into his drink. "Talking to people."

"Really? For as friendly as you are, I figured you'd have a lot of practice making small talk."

He laughs lightly. "I'm actually terrible at it, if you can't tell. I can say hi and start a conversation, but I have no idea where to go from there."

I lean my elbows on the table. "Let's start over, then. Hi, I'm Taylor, your neighbor in 201."

He smiles, grateful for the olive branch. "Hi Taylor, I'm Logan. You're a fashion designer, right?"

"Yes. And you... ?"

"I'm an I.T. guy."

I grin. "I wondered if you did something with computers."

"Really? Why's that?"

"Well, you know how you picture fashion designers? You're what I picture a tech guy would be like."

He grimaces. "It's the glasses, isn't it?"

I tilt my head, appraising him. "Not just the glasses. It's... I don't know. You just look smart. Confident."

"Confident?" He sits back, surprised. "Now there's a word I'd never use to describe myself."

I take another sip from my oversized mug. "You don't think you're confident? You talk to me just about every day."

He shrugs. "That doesn't mean I'm confident. Just neighborly."

I sit back in my chair and cross my arms. "No one is neighborly in New York. Which reminds me, are you from Alabama or something?"

He frowns. "Alabama? No, California. Why?"

"Hm. I guess I pegged you for a Southerner, what with the chivalry and neighborliness and all."

He laughs, and a deep cleft forms in his chin when he smiles. He has a nice smile. "Well, almost. My mom's from Texas so that's where I get it." He lifts his brow. "You?"

"Colorado."

"Any family?"

"I have an older sister who lives there with her husband

and kids. My dad is gone, and I haven't talked to my mom in years. What about you?"

"It's just me and my mom. She's still in Cali."

Suddenly his phone rings—at least, I think it's his phone. The Imperial March starts playing from somewhere in the vicinity, and he scrambles in his pockets to pull out his phone. He glances at the screen and mutes the call. I raise my eyebrows.

"Star Wars fan?" I ask.

He grins at me a little sheepishly. "Yeah. You?"

I shake my head. "Not really, but I know enough to get by. Definitely not enough to have the Rebel Alliance theme as my ringtone."

He chuckles, and I lean forward, resting my arms on the table. "So when you're not staring at a screen—because I assume you're a gamer, too—what else do you like to do?" I ask.

"I'm actually *not* a gamer, I'll have you know," he says, adjusting his glasses again. "I like to... um," he pauses, just long enough to make me curious. "I have other hobbies," he says quickly. "And I'm an amateur horticulturist."

"Other hobbies?"

"I like plants," he says in a deadpan voice. "That's my hobby."

"But you said other hobbies *and* a horticulturist." I squint my eyes at him, giving him a playful smile. "You don't dress up like a stormtrooper and go to Comic-Cons, do you?"

I catch him just as he's taking a sip of his tea and he chokes, coughing to catch his breath.

"That," he finally manages to gasp, his eyes full of laughter, "is not at all what I was expecting you to say." He continues to cough and laugh by turns until I grow concerned.

"Are you okay? Do you need some water?"

He nods, still sputtering, and I go up to the counter to ask for a cup of water. I take it back to our table and hand it to him.

"Remind me not to make jokes about your hobbies in the future," I say, when he finally looks somewhat in control.

"Remind me not to drink anything when we're having a conversation," he says, still raspy. His eyes are watering.

While Logan is fighting for breath, it dawns on me how much better I'm feeling. Having this random conversation with my almost-stranger-neighbor is exactly what I needed, apparently. Maybe Logan is right. Maybe I *do* need a friend.

Logan clears his throat a few more times, taking sips of water. Finally he looks up at me, his eyes full of amusement instead of tears. "Well, I'm done talking about myself. What about you? What do you like to do when you're not working?"

I shrug. "Nothing, really. Read fashion magazines, stalk designers on Instagram and TikTok, make my plans for world domination. You know, the usual."

"So you *do* want to be a runway designer?"

"Sure, doesn't everyone? I mean, Totsworth pays the bills and that's great, but no one enters the industry wanting to design onesies for a living. We all dream of the runway."

He nods. "I guess that makes sense. I just never thought about it before."

"Unless you're in the industry, I don't think many people do." I finish the last of my cappuccino and set my mug on the table.

"I actually know a bit about the fashion industry myself," he says, swirling the last of his tea.

I grin, raising my eyebrows at him. "Oh, really?"

He hears the challenge in my voice and sits back, a smug smile on his face. "Really."

"So is Imperial fashion your hobby, then? Black helmets, leather gloves, sweeping cloaks?" I ask.

He laughs, loud and long. It's contagious, and I find myself laughing with him.

"Taylor," he says, wiping tears from the corners of his eyes, "for someone who claims *not* to be a Star Wars fan, you certainly bring it up a lot."

"Sorry," I say, still grinning. "I couldn't help myself."

I glance outside for the first time since our arrival, and I'm surprised to see it's already getting dark. Did I really just spend an hour, laughing and talking with my neighbor?

Logan notices my look and offers a smile. "Ready to get going?"

Logan walks on the street-side of the sidewalk as we head back to our apartment building. I glance up at him and realize he's taller than I originally thought—closer to six foot than my own five-seven. He catches me looking at him and clears his throat.

"So what do you say, Taylor... um..." He frowns. "I guess I don't know your last name."

"O'Neill."

"Taylor O'Neill." He glances at my auburn hair and grins. "Irish, right?"

I roll my eyes. "Somewhere, at some point. My great-great-grandparents or something."

We arrive at the apartment building, where he unlocks the door and holds it open for me. I thank him and start up the stairs.

"Alright, Taylor O'Neill," he says, following me. "Now that

we've had coffee and you know I'm just a nerdy I.T. guy, what do you say? Friends?"

We get to the second floor landing—my apartment is on the left while his is on the right. I step toward my door and turn around, biting my lip.

"I don't know, Logan," I say, and his face falls. "I mean, I don't even know *your* last name."

His smile returns, deepening the cleft in his chin. "Alexander. Logan Alexander."

I nod, looking thoughtful. "Hmm. Logan Alexander, from California. An I.T. guy by day and *not* a Stormtrooper fashionista by night, who doesn't drink, likes plants, and has *other hobbies*." I raise an eyebrow at him, and he chuckles.

"That's right," he says.

"I might change my mind depending on those other hobbies, you know."

He sighs dramatically and takes off his glasses. Wiping them with the hem of his shirt, he says, "Yeah, but if you ghost me now, you might never find out what I know about the fashion industry."

I laugh. "You were just teasing me. You don't know anything about the fashion industry!"

"Don't I?"

He can't be serious... but he certainly *sounds* serious. He smiles, and when he places his glasses back on his face he gives me a wink. "G'night, Taylor O'Neill. It was nice to finally meet you."

"Wait, what do you know about the fashion industry?" I say.

But he just laughs, unlocks his door, and waves as he goes inside.

Chapter 3

I get up early the next morning, hoping to sneak into the office and get to work before too many others arrive. I'll be putting in some long hours if Greg wants the new collection before the end of next week, and I'm anxious to get started.

When I leave my apartment, I half expect to see Logan on the landing waiting for me, but he's not, of course. I'm surprised how disappointed I feel.

Turning around to lock my door, I see a pale yellow sticky note fluttering just above the handle. It says "Logan" with his phone number scrawled underneath.

I smile. Figures he'd have messy handwriting.

I grab a coffee to go from the same café we sat in the night before and head to the subway. On the way to work, I plug in Logan's number on my phone, making a mental note to text him later.

There's only one other person at work by the time I arrive, and she's sequestered in her cubicle as well. Good—I have a lot to do.

I spend the next hour going through Totsworth &

Company's Christmas collections from the last five years. They're all green, red, and black, usually with gold accents. Heritage plaid, velvet, taffeta—old school and boring. A wave of frustration rises up inside me. Why do they insist on doing the same thing in the same way, over and over again? Fashions and trends come and go like the weather, and if the company won't ever take risks they're never going to grow beyond their current market.

I take a sip of my coffee, and it reminds me of Logan and our non-date last night. Picking up my phone, I send him a quick text.

TAYLOR

Thanks again for last night. It was fun to get to know you a little better ☺

This is Taylor btw

I set the phone down and glumly look back at my computer screen. Heaving a sigh, I pull up the design software and start adjusting my collection.

After a few minutes, my phone buzzes beside me with an alert. I ignore it for a moment as I modify the color of the dress I'm working on, but then I pick it up. It's a reply from Logan.

LOGAN

Wait, which Taylor? I went out with two Taylors last night...

I smile, typing a quick reply with my thumbs.

TAYLOR

The one who called you a Stormtrooper

19

I turn back to my work, but pick up my phone as soon as it pings.

LOGAN

So not the one with the beard?

I laugh outright, covering my mouth when it comes out louder than I anticipated. He's funny. I didn't expect that, either.

I silence my phone and get back to work, feeling somehow lighter. I get most of the pieces put together in the new collection and I'm working on the fabric when I glance at the clock and see that it's time for lunch.

Wow, that was a productive morning. I pick up my phone to put in a Door Dash order and see a text from my sister.

RACHEL

Hey sis! I've got some exciting news. Call me when you get a chance, k?

I frown. What news? Her youngest is only a year old so I doubt it's another baby. I place my order for lunch and then text my sister back.

TAYLOR

I'm on lunch—should I call you now or wait till after work?

My phone rings a minute later, my sister's face lighting up my screen. "Hey Rach," I say, answering the call.

"Hey! How are you?"

"I'm alright. You?"

"Uh-oh, I know that tone. What's going on?"

I swivel in my chair, checking to see if anyone's around. "I showed my new collection to the team yesterday."

"The winter collection? I loved that one! What did they think?"

"Greg wants me to redo it. Make it more traditional."

"What? Why?"

I sigh. "He said it's too different and not worth the risk."

"That's ridiculous."

"I agree." I blow out my breath. "Anyways, what's your news?"

She squeals. "Marc just accepted a job in New Jersey— we're moving!"

My jaw drops open. "You're kidding. When? Why didn't you tell me sooner? Rachel!"

She laughs, and it feels like a hug. "I didn't want to get your hopes up, so I didn't tell you when he applied for the job."

"You're really moving out here? Where will he be working?"

"The Beth Israel Medical Center, in Newark."

"That's fantastic!" I say. I haven't lived near my sister in almost a decade. She met her husband, Marcos, while he was attending medical school in Denver. But once I graduated high school I went off to college in Pennsylvania, and then on to New York. I've missed her. Even though she's four years older than me, she's been my best friend for as long as I can remember. It will be great to have her close by again.

"So when do you think you'll move?" I ask.

"I'm not exactly sure—sometime this summer. Marc gave the hospital his 90 days' notice, and he starts his new job on July 5th. I'm hoping we can sell the house and find someplace to live before then so we can all move together, but we'll have to see how it all shakes out."

"Do you need help packing? Or watching the kids? Once I get this new collection finished I could take a few days off and come help you."

She laughs. "You have *never* liked babysitting, Taylor. Which means you're so excited you're not thinking straight."

I smile. "I *am* excited. I've missed you."

"I've missed you, too." My three-year-old niece starts screaming in the background, and she sighs. "Hey, I've got to go."

"Sounds like it. Thanks for the news—let me know if there's anything I can do to help, okay?"

"I will. Love you!"

"Love you, too."

I hang up the phone, grinning like the Cheshire cat. Who cares if I have to redo my collection—*my sister is moving to Jersey!* She came to visit me when I moved here a few years ago, before Grace was born. We went to museums and restaurants, saw the Statue of Liberty and Ground Zero, and got tickets on Broadway. We ate far too much food, spent far too much money, and stayed up far too late at night. I loved every minute of it.

But then I got busy with work and she got busy with her family, and time slipped away. I try to visit her in Colorado as often as I can, but that's never more than once or twice a year.

But now—*now!*—we can go ice skating at Rockefeller Center, take walks in Central Park, and maybe we can even find a yoga studio somewhere between us where we can meet up for class a couple times per week.

The thought carries me through the rest of the long afternoon.

It's almost seven when I finally call it a day, stretching my arms overhead and rolling out my neck. Oof. I haven't sat through such a long work day in months, and my back is feeling it.

I want to search up real estate listings to send my sister on the train, but without wifi I have to settle for the latest issue of Vogue, which I downloaded last week. My stop comes sooner than I expect, and before long I'm taking the stairs up to my apartment.

Flipping on the lights, I hang my keys by the door and pry off my shoes. I drop onto the couch, heaving a sigh as I close my eyes. A soak or a stretch? My muscles protest even the thought of getting up, but I know I'll regret it tomorrow if I don't do something to work out the kinks tonight. Better make it yoga— my muscles are stiff and tight from sitting at my desk all day, and I'm too keyed up about the news from my sister to relax in the tub.

I change into a pair of pajamas rather than my workout clothes, and sit down in the middle of my mat. I close my eyes and take a few deep, calming breaths, trying to bring my awareness to the present moment, noticing how my body feels, willing it to relax.

A thought darts into my brain, bright and beautiful, like a lightning bolt: *my sister is coming!* And not just for a visit, she's *moving* here. In just a few short months, she'll be sitting on the mat beside me in some backstreet studio, long hair pulled into a messy bun, reaching up toward the ceiling in the perfect side plank.

The thought makes me smile.

Chapter 4

I spend the weekend searching up real estate listings, sending my sister links to the most promising ones. She texts me back every time, sending laughing emojis at my exuberance, but I can tell she's just as excited as I am.

Monday morning comes sooner than I anticipate, and since I'm running late I don't have time to grab a coffee before work. Once I arrive at the office, I set my things down on my desk, turn on my computer, and head to the break room.

"Oh, hey Taylor. You're here early," Jeff says as I grab a mug from the cupboard. Jeff was one of the few coworkers who liked my designs and showed support for my winter collection.

"Yeah, I have to get the adjusted collection to Greg by the end of the week. I need all the time I can get." I pick up the coffeepot, filling my mug with liquid life.

He frowns. "I'm sorry it didn't pan out. I thought your collection was amazing."

I give him a small smile. "Thanks, I appreciate it."

"Do you need any help?"

"I don't think so," I say, adding cream and sugar to my cup and stirring it gently, "but I'll let you know if I do."

"Please do. Cheers," he says, raising his cup at me and walking out of the room.

I take my own mug back to my desk, sipping the steaming liquid as I walk. I can practically hear my neurons waking up as I swallow.

I've been able to transfer the overall designs from my Winter Wonderland collection to the new, adjusted one. For the most part I just needed to change the color palette, but there are a few pieces I have to adjust as well—things that won't look as good with solid organza as they would with a shimmery, iridescent one. I focus on green and gold, keeping red just as an accent, with some dark, chocolate brown accessories thrown in instead of the traditional black. I'm calling the new collection Winter Woodland, and hope that Greg approves.

I have a productive morning, and just before lunch my phone pings. I pick it up, expecting a text from my sister, but it's from Logan.

> **LOGAN**
>
> I know you're at work, but call me on your lunch break, I have a proposition for you.
>
> If you want to
>
> But it's cool if you don't

I grin. He's so awkward it's adorable.

I put in an online order for the deli down the street, then tap Logan's name to give him a call. It rings twice before he picks up.

"Hey, Taylor," he says.

"Hey, Logan. I hear you have a proposition for me."

"Yep."

"Does it involve your other hobbies? Because I've been thinking about that, and I have some new theories."

He sighs. "You're not going to let that go, are you?"

"Nope." I pop the P, grinning.

"Well, sorry to disappoint you, but not today. Although it does involve my plants."

"Plants aren't nearly as interesting as secret hobbies."

"Wouldn't it depend on the hobby, though? Plants can be very interesting."

"You sound like my ninth grade biology teacher."

He laughs. "Fair enough. Anyway, do you want to know what my proposition is?"

"Sure, let's hear it."

"Remember how I told you I knew a little about the fashion industry?"

"Yeah..."

"Well, if you meet me for dinner tonight, I'll tell you all about it. Deal?"

I bite my lip. Chatting with my neighbor over coffee felt innocent enough, but meeting Logan in the evening for dinner *definitely* feels like a date. And my spreadsheet still doesn't have room for a relationship.

I hesitate long enough that he speaks again. "If it would help you decide, dinner would consist of meeting me on the roof for takeout. Nothing fancy."

"We have roof access?"

"Yeah, didn't you know?" His voice kicks up a notch with excitement. "Ok, now you *have* to meet me. The view is amazing." When I still don't answer, he adds, "We can scrap the dinner plans if you'd like. Just a couple neighbors checking out the view."

"You're really stubborn, you know that?"

"I prefer tenacious," he says, and I chuckle. "So what do you say?"

My phone alerts me that my lunch order is ready for pickup, which is my cue to wrap things up. "Alright, I'll meet you on the roof. But no dinner. How do I get up there?"

"Just knock on my door whenever you're ready and I'll take you up. See you tonight!"

"See ya."

I hang up the phone, my stomach twisting into knots. It isn't the fact that I'm meeting my neighbor for another not-quite-date that has me nervous, it's the fact that I'm actually looking forward to it.

What have I gotten myself into?

———

We didn't specify a time to meet, but since Logan initially mentioned dinner, I assume six or seven is good. I contemplate staying in my work clothes, but since I'm wearing high heels and a pants suit, it feels a little too formal and that would *definitely* make it feel like a date. Instead, I slip into my favorite jeans and a white T-shirt, then head over to Logan's apartment. I knock on the door and wait, feeling awkward and self-conscious, wondering if I really should have agreed to this at all.

Logan answers the door wearing Chuck Taylors and a grin. "Hey neighbor, come on in."

I hesitate. "Oh, is now not a good time? I can come back..."

"No, it's fine, I just need to pull something out of the oven."

He disappears around the corner while I wait outside the door. He returns in a minute and I step back onto the landing as he locks his door.

"Something smells good," I say. "What are you making?"

"One of my specialties: Stouffer's lasagna. You sure you don't want some?"

I smile. "I'm good, but thanks. So how do we get onto the roof?"

Logan grins. "It's the best kept secret this place has," he says. "You're gonna love it."

"Is it even allowed?"

He scoffs. "Do I look like the kind of guy who'd do something that wasn't allowed? Come on."

We head upstairs to the third floor, and then the fourth floor, and then the fifth floor. "This building is a lot higher than I realized," I huff, finally stepping out onto the fifth floor landing. Only it isn't a landing, it's the end of a long hallway. "Huh. I didn't know this was up here."

"Yup. It's like the hall on the ground floor, meant to connect the two ends of the building," Logan says. "This way."

I follow him down the hall, stopping in front of a heavy door with a sign that says AUTHORIZED PERSONNEL ONLY. I raise an eyebrow at him.

"It's fine," he says. "I talked to the building manager about it months ago. We're definitely allowed."

I shake my head as he opens the door for me. "If we get arrested I'm never speaking to you again," I say, starting up another, shorter set of stairs.

"It's not even locked," Logan says from behind me as we climb. "If we weren't allowed, would the door be unlocked?"

There's a tiny landing with another door at the top of the

stairs. I turn the handle and push the door out, stepping up onto the roof.

The roof is basically flat—a long rectangle divided roughly in half by the door we came up out of. On one side of the roof are four raised garden beds, and on the other side of the roof are a few pieces of mismatched outdoor furniture and a small table, with a few flowerpots scattered here and there.

"Welcome to the top of the world," Logan says, spreading his arms wide.

"Wow. You weren't kidding about the view," I say, walking closer to the edge of the roof. Dozens of treetops from the park across the street spread out in a sea of pale green before me. At their center, the Martyr's Monument reaches above the canopy like a beacon, drawing the eye to the weathered lantern at its tip. Beyond the park, the buildings of downtown Brooklyn stretch heavenward, and even farther away, across the wide river and more to the north, the skyscrapers of Manhattan crowd together like jagged, glistening jewels.

It's breathtaking.

"Beautiful, isn't it?" Logan says, coming to stand beside me. "It was the biggest selling point for me when I was looking at the apartment."

"I had no idea," I say. "They either didn't mention it or I wasn't paying attention."

I lean my elbows on the low wall and look down the street. It's starting to get dark so the park is basically empty, though a few pedestrians walk along the road. A light breeze tickles my nose, bringing with it the smell of coffee and curry from the nearby restaurants. I take a deep breath in, smelling car exhaust and—if I close my eyes and concentrate—the fishy scent of the sea.

"Well, here we are," I say, opening my eyes and looking at Logan significantly. He chuckles and turns around, making his way to one of the lounge chairs, and I follow. By the time I sit down and look at him he's grinning like a kid in a candy store, and I can't help but grin back, even as I raise an eyebrow at him. "After all this hype, it had better be good," I say.

"Oh, it is," he says, pushing his glasses back up his face. He leans over. "The reason I know about fashion is because I work for Vince Milton."

A laugh bursts out of me before I can stop it. "The TikTok king? No way."

Logan leans back. "The very same," he says, looking smug.

"I thought you said you were an I.T. guy?"

"I am—I'm a freelancer. I have a few different clients that I do various jobs for, but Vince is my biggest."

"I don't know," I say, still skeptical. "That's a pretty bold claim."

Bold doesn't really even cover it. Vince Milton, aka Emperor365, is one of the biggest social media influencers in the country. He's one of those celebrities without real cause for being a celebrity, other than having exceptional good looks and enough money to run a small country. He's a trust-child—his family are behind the Milton Resorts empire.

Logan shrugs, unaffected by my skepticism. "Believe it or not, it's the truth."

"What kind of I.T. work do you do for him?" I'm still not convinced, but it seems the polite thing to ask.

"Photo and video editing mostly. Some web design. Stuff like that."

"Wait, what? You edit his photos and videos? Like for Instagram and TikTok?"

"Yeah. Vince has a photographer who does a lot of work as well, but the candid shots and videos Vince takes himself. But he's too busy—or perhaps lazy—to turn it into usable content, so I put the reels and montages together for him."

"That doesn't sound much like I.T. work."

A hint of pink creeps up Logan's neck. "Yeah, I know. I started out as just the web guy. But as his popularity grew, so did my responsibilities." He shrugs. "I kind of learned all the other stuff on the job."

I raise an eyebrow at him, and his blush deepens. "It pays the bills," he says, echoing what I said to him about my own job.

But it still sounds surreal. Could my charmingly nerdy neighbor be part of such an exclusive, elite team? I know a handful of designers who'd give their right arm for a chance to work with Vince Milton, myself included. He attends all the biggest events and galas, and has earned himself a following of more than 300 million fans. He's become a household name synonymous with the best and newest of everything. From flora to fashion and entertainment to electronics, if he likes something, stocks and sales skyrocket, and if he doesn't... well. Let's just say there's a reason Art & Sole Shoes aren't around anymore.

"So how's the redesign going?"

Logan's question pulls me out of my thoughts. "Good. I should have it finished in a few days."

"You don't sound particularly pleased about it."

I shrug. "It's fine. It's more in line with what my boss wants, so that's what matters."

"But is it what *you* want?"

I laugh humorlessly. "Not really. It's predictable and boring, which are two things I loathe. I became a designer because I wanted to create new, exciting clothes and accessories, and this collection is anything but." I sigh, looking out over the rooftops.

Logan looks out at the view with me. The sun is dipping lower and the sky is turning pink around the edges. A flock of pigeons bursts upwards from somewhere down the street, streaking across the horizon and disappearing into the distance.

"I'm sorry about your boss," Logan says. "He should have gone with your original collection."

I smile. "That's very kind of you to say. But you haven't even seen my designs—how do you know they weren't terrible?"

"Good point," he laughs. "Have you got some pics?"

I wave him off. "I was kidding."

"But I wasn't," he says. "I'd really like to see them."

"It's just a bunch of boring kids clothes. You wouldn't be interested."

He frowns. "You said you hated boring."

"I mean boring for you. You don't have any kids, do you?"

"No."

"So why would you want to see a bunch of kids' clothes?"

"Because you designed them," he says, as if it's the most obvious thing in the world. "And you're my friend. Friends share things and support one another, you know?"

I grimace. "You sure you want to see it?"

"Absolutely."

I sigh, pulling out my phone. A few taps and swipes and then I hand it over to him. "That's the collection I originally designed. You can swipe through to see it all."

Logan takes my phone and adjusts his glasses. I turn away so I don't have to watch his face while he looks at it, suddenly nervous about his opinion. I mean, he works for Vince Milton, for goodness sake. He's got to have *some* kind of taste.

I don't wait in suspense very long. "Dang, Taylor," he says, after scrolling for just a few moments. "These are amazing."

"You like it?" I say, my lips pulling into a grin.

"The collection is stunning," he says, handing the phone back to me. "You ever thought about working for a big house?"

"I'd love to," I say. "But it's hard to get a shoe in. I apply for every opening I find, and occasionally I get an interview."

"But nothing yet," Logan finishes for me.

I smile and lift a shoulder. "Not yet. But I'll get there, someday. Just need some patience and experience. And Totsworth can get me by until then."

We sit in silence as the sky darkens overhead. A sea of multi-colored stars grows around us, each one a light from a home or car or traffic signal. I tip my head back, seeing far fewer stars above me. The air grows chilly and I shiver, getting to my feet.

"Your lasagna's probably cold by now," I say to Logan, who also stands.

He shrugs. "Nothing a microwave can't fix."

I laugh lightly. "That's true. Well, thanks for inviting me to join you tonight."

"You're welcome. It's kind of fun to have a toe in the same industry."

"It is. And it's beautiful up here," I say, my eyes sweeping across the horizon. "I'll have to make time to enjoy it."

"If you ever want some company, just let me know," he says, digging his hands into his pockets.

I smile. "I will."

Chapter 5

I don't see or hear from Logan again for a few days. I'm equal parts disappointed and relieved—disappointed because I want to see him, and relieved because I shouldn't want to see him. I'm already distracted at work thinking about his smile and quirky sense of humor, and I can*not* afford distractions.

I turn in my new collection to Greg on Friday, and he loves it. His praise grates on my nerves, though. There's nothing really unique or interesting about the collection; nothing about it says *Taylor O'Neill designed this*. Why can't he acknowledge and appreciate my own style?

When I get back to my desk, I have two missed calls and a text from Logan. I pull up his message, trying to ignore the giddy excitement I feel.

LOGAN

Call me asap, I need your help

His message surprises me. What does he need my help with? And why is it so urgent?

I glance at the clock—5:13. There's only fifteen minutes left of the work day...

I set my phone down, determined to wait until after work to call him. *Boundaries*, I tell myself. *If you respond now, he'll think you're waiting by the phone to hear from him. It can wait.*

But I can't focus. No matter how hard I try to concentrate on my work, my mind keeps wandering and my eyes keep traveling to my phone. I put it inside a drawer and feel a small measure of relief, trying again to focus on my work.

"You're still here?"

I look up to see Greg standing just outside my cubicle.

"I figured you'd head out after our meeting," he says. "I know you put in extra hours to get that collection to me on time —get out of here. Enjoy your weekend."

He smiles and waves, and I wave back. Excitement and nerves course through me as I think about talking with Logan. Shutting down my computer, I gather my things and head for the elevator. Not until I'm outside the building do I pull up Logan's number and call.

He answers on the first ring. "Taylor! Oh I'm so glad you called back. Vince wants to meet you—can you make it to *The Nightingale* by six?"

I freeze on the sidewalk, because there's no way I heard him correctly. "I'm sorry, what?"

"Can you meet me and Vince at *The Nightingale* by 6 o'clock?"

Slowly I start walking again. I guess I did hear him right. "Why on earth does Vince Milton want to meet me?" I pause, my stomach dropping to my knees. "Is this just another one of your tricks to get me to have dinner with you?"

"I don't have time to explain everything to you, but it's not a trick, I swear. This is urgent, Taylor. *Can you meet us by six?*"

"Um..." My mind is a jumble. How does Vince Milton even know my name? What has Logan said about me?

I glance at my watch. 5:22. I've passed the restaurant several times when I've been shopping in that part of Manhattan, and there's no way I'll make it on foot. I sigh.

"Yeah, I can meet you, but I'm coming straight from work."

"Brilliant, let me talk to Vince and I'll call you soon to explain."

He hangs up before I can even say goodbye.

There isn't time to call an Uber, so I head for the edge of the street, my nerves turning to annoyance as I look for a car. Contrary to popular belief, cabs aren't roaming the streets of New York in yellow-checkered packs like you see in all the old sitcoms—I usually need to call ahead when I need a car. But fate must be smiling down on me, because I see one pull up in front of the office building next door. The back door opens and a balding gentleman steps out.

"Hold the cab!" I holler, raising my arm and hurrying down the sidewalk. The man sees me, then ducks his head inside to say something to the driver before stepping back and shutting the door. The car doesn't pull away, so I'm assuming he told the driver to wait.

Bless him. I hope he believes in karma.

"*The Nightingale* on 10th, in the Village," I say, climbing inside.

The driver nods. "You got it," he says, maneuvering back into traffic.

I wrack my brain as I catch my breath, going over every conversation Logan and I have had, trying to figure out what he may have told Vince about me. Why does he want to meet me? Is he thinking of launching a children's clothing line? My stomach churns with anxiety until Logan calls a few minutes later.

"If this turns out to be a hoax, I'm billing you for my cab fare," I say as I answer the phone. The driver glances at me in the rear view mirror but says nothing.

Logan chuckles. "It's not a hoax. Vince's personal designer just quit and he's freaking out. The Met Gala is in three weeks and she took her designs with her, so he doesn't have anything to wear. I told him I knew a designer who might be able to help him, and he wants to meet you."

I hear the words, but my brain can't process them. I'm about to meet Vince Milton—THE Vince Milton—and possibly create an ensemble for him to wear to the Met Gala?

"Taylor? You there?"

"Yeah, I just..." I rub my temple, reminding myself to breathe. My heart is racing and I'm pretty sure my blood pressure is higher than the Empire State Building at this point. I manage a shaky laugh. "It's a lot to take in, you know?"

"Yeah."

I take a deep breath. "So Vince Milton wants to meet me."

"Yes."

"And he needs an outfit designed for the Met Gala in three weeks."

"Yes."

"Because his personal designer just quit? Why?"

"I'm not sure, honestly. I don't deal much with that side of things so I have no idea what happened. All I know is that Vince sent out a mass text to the team telling us he needs a new designer immediately."

"So this won't be just a one-time gig? He's looking to hire someone full-time?"

"I assume so. Vince likes having a personal designer basically at his beck and call. He has a whole team of seamstresses to make whatever his designer creates, and I don't have to tell you that money isn't an issue."

"Right."

"Taylor," Logan says, and I hear a note of hesitancy in his voice, "Vince can be... well, a bit of a diva."

I almost snort a laugh, but stop myself just in time. "I've gathered that from his social media posts."

"You follow him online?"

"Of course. It's my job to keep my finger on the pulse of fashion, and that means following all the biggest names. Including Vince Milton."

"Good, he'll like that. Do you have your portfolio with you, or access to it digitally?"

"I didn't have time to grab it, but I have an online portfolio."

"Perfect, will you text me a link? I can send it to Vince so he can take a look at it before you arrive."

A bubble of hope starts growing inside me. This could be it. This could be my big break, the step up I need to launch my career as a real fashion designer.

"I'll text you a link as soon as we end the call," I say. "Anything else I should know?"

"I think that's it. Just be yourself and answer honestly, because your work will speak for itself."

"Got it."

"Good luck," Logan says. "See you soon."

———

The car drops me off outside the restaurant five minutes before six. I give myself a quick once-over, making sure I'm as put together as possible before taking a breath and opening the door.

The Nightingale is a posh little place I've seen but never been into before. I give my name to the maitre'd, and he takes me to a secluded table in the far corner. Logan sees us coming and jumps up, offering me an encouraging smile.

"Taylor, so glad you could make it," he says. He turns to the man sitting across the table. "Vince, this is Taylor O'Neill. Taylor, Vince Milton."

Vince reaches out a ring-studded hand to shake mine. "I've heard so much about you from Logan here," he says, flicking his chin at my neighbor. "Please, join us."

Logan holds the chair for me like he did in the café. "Thank you," I say, too nervous for any sort of quip. He smiles and takes his seat again, and I turn my attention to the man lounging in the seat beside him.

Vince Milton looks exactly how he looks online. He's posted thousands of photos and videos of himself from all angles, so I feel as though I know his face as well as my own. Thick, dark hair hangs in artfully styled waves to his shoulders, which are narrow on his tall frame. He has a full beard that is nicely trimmed, and startling blue eyes that surprise me. I always assumed he amped up the vibrance in the photos, but his eyes really are incredibly blue.

"Miss O'Neill—can I call you Taylor?" I open my mouth to reply, but he continues before I can answer. "I had a chance to look at your portfolio, and while not expansive, it was certainly impressive." Vince takes a sip from his wine glass and I smile, trying not to let the thrill I feel at his words give me too much confidence. "Your style is bold and unique, fresh and enlightening. I'm positively thrilled to have discovered you."

My eyes dart to Logan, who gives me a smile and the tiniest nod. Apparently he doesn't mind his boss taking credit for Logan's share in that discovery.

"As I'm sure Logan has made you aware, I've found myself in a tight spot. The Met Gala is in three weeks and I have nothing to wear."

I sit up a bit straighter, knowing what's coming but still not wanting to miss anything he says.

"You obviously have talent," he continues, "but as I understand it, you're not getting much opportunity to stretch your wings with your current employer." He lifts an eyebrow at me expectantly.

"That's correct," I say. "I'm a designer for Totsworth & Company, and I—"

"I'm not at all interested in what work you do now," he says, cutting me off with an impatient flick of his wrist. "What I'm interested in is what work you can do for *me*."

Logan offers me an apologetic little smile when I once again glance his way. Apparently this is the sort of thing he meant when he warned me that Vince Milton could be a bit of a diva. Arrogant jerk would have been a better description, but he's practically fashion royalty—I guess he's used to getting away with it.

"What did you have in mind?" I ask, lacing my fingers together and resting my hands on the table.

"As fascinating as you must find your current work," he says, his voice dripping with sarcasm, "with a talent like yours, I'm sure you dream of the runway." He pauses, and I nod.

Satisfied, he continues. "I can help you get there, if you can help me in the meantime."

He sits up, suddenly business-like, his blue eyes boring into my green ones across the table. "Design me a show-stopping ensemble for the Met Gala, and if I'm satisfied with your work, I'll bring you on as my personal designer."

And there it is. His offer sits in front of me like the most tantalizing steak, mouthwatering and rare. I want it—oh, how I want it! But there's something I need to know first.

I clear my throat a little. "Can you tell me what happened with your previous designer?"

I can tell from the way Vince's eyes narrow that my question isn't welcome. Logan looks uneasy, his wide eyes sending me a silent warning.

"Let's just say her sense of fashion was no longer in sync with my own," Vince says, his voice dangerously smooth. I nod slowly, trying to ignore the unease growing in my gut.

It's clear that Vince expects me to accept his offer, and I can sense that if I leave the restaurant without giving him an answer, I leave the opportunity behind with me. I take a deep breath, willing myself to feel the confidence I lack.

"Noted," I say. "When do you need the designs?"

From the corner of my eye I see Logan relax. Vince sits back, oozing charm and ease once more.

"My staff is used to working on a deadline and will only require a week or two to finalize and fit my clothing, provided the materials requested are available to them. I'll put you in touch with Amelia—she can tell you what they do and don't have on hand."

I nod.

"I look forward to seeing what you come up with." Vince's smile turns acidic. "Let's hope it doesn't disappoint."

Chapter 6

Vince doesn't stay; after he finishes his drink he excuses himself and leaves the restaurant. Well, I guess he doesn't really excuse himself —he just drains his glass, stands up, and walks away. It alarms me at first, but Logan shrugs it off, assuring me it's normal behavior and inviting me to stay and have dinner with him.

"It's on Vince's tab, so we may as well eat, right?" he says with a grin.

I narrow my eyes at him. "I knew this was just a ploy to get me to have dinner with you." He rolls his eyes and I laugh lightly. "Alright, I guess dinner couldn't hurt. We're business colleagues now, aren't we?" *Which makes this a business dinner,* not *a date,* I silently tell myself.

My nerves start to settle as I look over the menu. "Have you been here before?" I ask. "Anything you'd recommend?"

He nods. "A handful of times, but I'd rather not recommend anything."

"Oh? Why not?"

"Well, you can tell a lot about a woman by the food they order. I'm curious to see what you'll choose."

I arch an eyebrow at him. "And you've been gathering this data for how long?"

He grimaces. "Let's just say I've been on a *lot* of first dates."

I smirk. "So what does it tell you if I order a salad?"

"Oh no, please don't order a salad," he groans.

"Why not?"

"Because most women order salad. But why? Are they on a diet? Did they eat before they came? Are they self-conscious about how much food they consume in front of others? I don't know what it all means, but if a woman orders a salad, I know she's got issues. Who orders a salad instead of a steak when someone else is paying?"

"A vegetarian," I deadpan.

"But what if I know my date isn't a vegetarian?"

I roll my eyes. "It couldn't possibly be because she *likes* salad, could it?"

"Of course not. Women who order salad on a first date have issues."

"This isn't a date."

"You know what I mean," he says, waving a hand dismissively.

I fold my arms across my chest, amused. I know he isn't serious—that playful grin he keeps shooting me assures me of that—but I'm curious to see what he's getting at.

"So most women order a salad on the first date, huh?"

"In my experience, yes."

"And that's it? That tells you she's got issues, so you're not interested?"

"Pretty much. But if a woman orders a steak," he says, lifting his brow, "I'll definitely ask her for a second date."

I scoff. "Just because she orders a steak?"

"Sure. If a woman orders a steak, I know she's confident. She's not afraid of what the guy is going to think of her, because he's going to order a steak, too. She sees herself as his equal, and that," he sits back with a smug smile, "is the kind of woman I like."

"And what if she orders lobster?"

"Oh, lobster," he says, rolling his eyes dramatically, and I can't help but laugh. "If a woman orders lobster, I know she's not interested. She just wants to milk me for all I'm worth and then ghost me after the night is over."

The waiter comes up just then and asks what I'd like. "I'll have the lobster and a six-ounce steak, please." I glance at Logan, who chuckles. I hand the menu to the waiter and add, "Throw in a side salad as well."

Logan orders (a twelve-ounce sirloin with two baked potatoes), and when the waiter walks away, I cock an eyebrow at him.

"And if a woman orders all three?" I ask. "What does that say about her?"

"It says she's either really hungry," he shrugs, "or she's a lesbian."

I burst out laughing, and several people nearby turn to look at us. I try to catch my breath, wiping at the tears that leak from my eyes. "Is this one of your other hobbies, then? Dating psychology?"

"Nah. I'm sure there's a psychology major somewhere who's analyzed this type of data, but this was just for fun. I just wanted to make you laugh."

I shake my head. "Mission accomplished, then. But I have to remind you that this isn't a date."

He huffs in exasperation. "I'm starting to get the impression you don't like dating, Taylor O'Neill from Colorado."

I lift my glass and take a sip. "No time for it, I'm afraid. Besides, I'm prejudiced against guys who order two potatoes."

The food is delicious, of course. Logan and I laugh and talk, sharing the things we like about living in New York City, and groaning over the stuff we don't. I'm surprised at how similar our feelings are about living here.

"What brought you to New York in the first place?" I ask him.

He shrugs. "It seemed as good a place as any. Besides, I heard some advice that everyone should live in New York at least once, but leave before it makes you hard. And to live in Southern California once, but leave before it makes you soft. Being born and raised in SoCal meant I was already pretty soft, so I figured I may as well see if living in New York could toughen me up."

"What was it like growing up in California? Are you a surfer?" Somehow I can't picture it, but I wonder if it's one of his *other hobbies*.

Logan shakes his head. "Why does everyone think that California is one big beach? And that everyone surfs there?"

"I don't know. I guess for the same reason people think that everyone from Colorado likes to ski."

"You don't like to ski?"

I grin. "Actually, I love it."

"Why am I not surprised."

"What about you? Do you like to ski?"

"Never been. And I don't surf, either. We actually didn't live on the coast, we were further inland."

There is a lull in our conversation, and I take the opportunity to check the time. It's already after eight.

"Ready to head out?" Logan asks, and I nod.

We share an Uber to get home, and as we climb the stairs to our respective apartments, I pause and look back at him.

"All that really happened tonight, right? With Vince Milton at *The Nightingale?*"

Logan smiles. "Yeah. Welcome to the big leagues, Taylor."

I let out a breathless laugh. "Hardly. But still... Vince Milton..." I shake my head and continue up the stairs.

I say goodnight and head inside my apartment. I don't often come home so late, and all the lights are out. I stand in the stillness for a moment, waiting for reality to sink in.

I'm going to design for Vince Milton.

I turn on the lights, pulling out my phone as I kick off my shoes. I speed dial my sister, the grin on my face growing with every ring. At last she answers.

"Hey Taylor, what's up?"

"You are never going to believe what just happened to me."

Chapter 7

I wake up to clear, spring sunshine streaming through my curtains. Rolling onto my back, I stare up at the ceiling, letting my fuzzy thoughts settle.

Suddenly I sit bolt upright. Grabbing my phone, I open my messages and pull up the convo with Logan. It's all there, even the late-night texts he sent after we got home, and I let my breath out in an exultant laugh, feeling giddy.

> **LOGAN**
>
> Thanks for staying to have dinner with me after Vince left. What'd you think of him IRL?

> **TAYLOR**
>
> He's certainly intimidating

> **LOGAN**
>
> That's the diva in him

It really happened, then. I'm actually going to design something for *Vince Milton!* It still doesn't feel real, but real or not, I have only a short time to pull something together, so I've got to get to work.

Every year the Met Gala has a theme, and this year the theme is "Renaissance." Ideas are already coursing through my head as I pull up my email. There's one from Vince's head seamstress Amelia, detailing the types and colors of fabric and trim they have on hand, as well as some specialty items they purchased in preparation for this year's event. She invites me to come tour the studio this afternoon, and I sigh with relief. Seeing the fabrics and notions in person will help immensely in the design process.

I send her a quick reply before hopping in the shower. Throwing on some jeans and a hoodie, I pull my hair into a messy bun. Auburn-colored curls stick out in unfettered delight as I grab a cup of coffee and my laptop bag.

I open the door onto the roof tentatively, still worried I'm not *actually* allowed up here. An older woman in a large sunhat is tending to some of the plants on the far side of the roof, but no one is lounging on the nearby patio furniture. Taking a seat in one of the padded chairs, I open up my computer.

I've been researching Renaissance art and fashion for an hour when I hear the door to the roof open behind me. I assume it's the gardener heading downstairs until I hear a familiar voice.

"Glad to see you're enjoying our view."

I turn to see Logan coming toward me with a mug in hand, and I smile.

"It's nicer than the one from my window.

He nods. "Mine, too. Mind if I join you?"

"Not at all."

Logan takes the chair beside me, the quiet settling between us like a blanket, warm and comfortable. We sit there for a time, sipping our drinks, the *tap, tap* of my keyboard occasionally broken by the scratching of pencil on my drawing pad as I take notes and sketch out some ideas.

After twenty minutes, Logan stands and stretches. He sets his empty cup on the small, glass-topped table and walks out of sight behind me. I glance over my shoulder to see him dragging a hose from the other side of the roof to where we've been sitting.

"What are you doing?"

"Watering my plants," he says, indicating the two large flowerpots to my right.

"These are *your* flowers?"

"Yep. Horticulturist, remember?"

The hose has a red nozzle attached to the end of it, and after clicking it into the correct position, he pulls the trigger and a shower of water cascades out. He douses one flowerpot and then the other, then hauls the hose to the other nearby pots.

"There," he says, after watering all the flowers and taking the hose back to the other side. "That should keep them happy for today."

"Do you have to water them every day?" I ask.

"Usually. When summer comes, I'll have to water them twice on most days. There's not really any shade up here, so they're all sun-loving plants. But the pots dry out quickly and the roots get hot, so I have to keep them damp."

I look at the large pot a few feet from my chair. Bright red geraniums sprout from the center of it, with delicate yellow flowers surrounding them. Something green with small, round, fan-like leaves trails down the sides.

"What's that green plant?" I ask, pointing to the pot.

"That's Creeping Jenny," Logan says. "It grows back almost every year."

"Does it have flowers?"

"No, but it's a good spiller."

"Spiller?"

"It spills down the sides. See," he says, going over to the pot, "good flowerpots will have three types of plants: thrillers, fillers, and spillers. The thrillers are big and placed in the center—the geraniums here. Fillers come next; they fill in the space between the center of the pot and the edges. And spillers are planted along the outside, so they spill down the sides."

"Wow. I had no idea there was a formula for flowerpots."

"Gardening is full of math," he says, taking his seat again. "Which is probably one of the reasons why I like it so much."

"Do you have a vegetable garden, too?" I say, hitching my thumb over my shoulder at the raised beds on the other side of the roof.

"Oh, no," he says with a laugh. "I can't cook at all. There wouldn't be any point."

I admire the flowers scattered around the rooftop. There's another pot similar to the large one he showed me, only the geraniums are a brilliant coral color. A smaller pot beside it is filled with small purple flowers, and another one near the wall is filled with those trumpet-like flowers in various hues (petunias, I think). The blossoms are bright and cheerful, and I smile as I look around.

"You know, I never would have pegged you for a flower guy," I say, giving Logan an appraising look.

He shrugs good-naturedly. "Most people don't."

"What got you interested in plants in the first place?"

He crosses his arms and leans back, placing his feet up on the low table in front of him. "I took a horticulture class in high school. We were required to take a lab science, and neither chemistry nor biology appealed to me. So I signed up for horticulture, thinking it might be boring but at least it'd be an easy A."

"And was it?"

"Boring? Or an easy A?"

"Either. Both."

"It was neither, actually," he says with a chuckle. "Not boring at all, and way more difficult than I anticipated. We were required to memorize both the Latin *and* the common names of over two hundred domestic flowers and plants. There were a couple huge greenhouses in the back of the school where we grew everything. We had a big plant sale in the spring, which meant we had to keep our plants alive all winter long if we wanted to sell anything and pass the class."

"Wow."

"Yeah. We learned flower arranging too, but those lessons never really took root." He looks at me expectantly.

I blink. "Did you... did you just make a plant joke?"

He grins. "Maybe."

I roll my eyes and turn back to my computer.

"Okay, fine, it was a lame joke. But can you blame me? The timing was perfect!"

I don't respond, but the corner of my mouth lifts in a smile.

"Speaking of flowers," he says, "have you ever been to the Orchid Show at the Botanical Garden?" he asks.

I look up. "No, but I've been hearing buzz about it—the theme this year is Florals in Fashion."

"We should go," Logan says. "I was planning to get tickets anyway, since I haven't been this year yet. Want to check it out together?"

"I don't know," I hedge. "I'm meeting Amelia at the studio

this afternoon, and I'd really like to get this design for Vince put together ASAP. And I'm still working full-time at Totsworth."

"How about next Sunday? That gives you a week to put something together for Vince, and plenty of time to come up with another excuse to decline going out with me."

"What!" I huff. "I do *not* give excuses."

He shrugs, but I catch his lips twitching. I narrow my eyes.

"Valid *reasons* for declining offers are completely different than excuses, Logan," I say, glaring at him.

He chuckles. "Fair enough. So what do you say—next Sunday?"

I pinch my lips together. "I should tell you no, just to teach you a lesson."

A wide grin splits his face. "Which would only prove my point."

"You're impossible," I grumble. "Fine. Next Sunday. But I'll buy my own ticket."

Logan laughs, holding up his hands. "Whatever you want, Taylor. I'm just glad you said yes." He gets to his feet and grabs his cup. "I better let you focus," he says with a smile. "Good luck with the design."

"Thanks."

"Will I get to see it before you send it off to Vince?"

I hesitate. "I don't usually share my preliminary designs..."

He smiles. "That's okay, I understand. See ya, Taylor."

"See ya."

I work for another hour on the roof and then head back to my apartment. By lunchtime I have a few tentative sketches of what I have in mind for the finished design, but I'll have to wait to flesh them out until after I see what I have to work with. Wanting to make a good impression, I choose my outfit carefully, dressing like I would for an interview. Smoothing my hair into a bun at the nape of my neck, I grab my keys and head out the door.

Amelia sent me the directions to the studio in an email, and at half past two I arrive. The address leads me to an unassuming door in a brick wall with nothing behind it but a set of stairs. Reaching the top, I can see that the studio takes up the entire second floor of the building. It's basically one massive room split into two main sections: one area for sewing and creating, and the other for taking photographs and videos. There's an eclectic, grungy feel to the space, which matches the aesthetic of Vince's online persona.

A middle-aged Hispanic woman notices me standing just inside the room, and she walks briskly over. "Unless you are Miss O'Neill, you shouldn't be here," she says, a slight accent tugging on her words.

"That's me," I say. "Taylor O'Neill. You must be Amelia."

Her eyes sweep over me, and I squirm under her gaze. "Hm," she says after a moment. "You're younger than I was expecting."

Logan's voice saying *I always pictured you as the next Coco Chanel* suddenly flits into my mind, making me stand a little taller. *Fake it till you make it,* I think to myself.

"Come," she calls, walking away from me. "Let me show you what we have."

She leads me across the room to a series of shelves stacked neatly with bolts of cloth. "The fabric is organized by type, and then color," she says, indicating the shelves with a sweep of her arm. "Cotton blends are here, linen and muslin are there, organza, velvet, and satins over there. Other fabrics are arranged by weight on the far shelves." I nod, noticing that each type of fabric is arranged in its own rainbow. I walk over to the linen and pull out a bolt, running my hand along the woven threads. It's tight and smooth; a high quality fabric. Amelia watches me for a moment, then indicates a large table to her right.

"You are welcome to use this table while you're here," she says. "It is rarely used by myself or the other seamstresses."

I nod. "And is that the trim, on the shelves behind you?"

She turns with a nod. "Yes. Each tub is carefully organized, so please do not pull things out if you're not exactly sure where to put it back," she says sharply. "Myself or one of the others can help you locate anything you need."

Her manner is brisk and efficient, and I wonder what it will be like to work with her. I ask a few more questions, taking notes on the fabric in stock and the specialty trims available. I request samples of a few things, and she has one of her assistants put them together for me. Before I leave, I summon the courage to ask her about the previous designer.

"Sorry," she says. "I'm under an NDA regarding the designers Vince works with—there's nothing I can say."

Her answer surprises me. Why would Vince require his head seamstress to sign a contract containing a gagging clause? Do *all* his employees have to sign such a contract?

"When would you like to come back?"

Amelia's question startles me out of my thoughts. "Oh. Um, how about Tuesday? Are you here in the evenings?"

She purses her lips. "You will not be back on Monday?"

I wilt at her tone. "Sorry, I have a day job. And I need some time to put together my ideas and run them past Vince—er, Mr. Milton."

"Hmm. Well. We do not usually work in the evenings. But

Mr. Milton told us to accommodate you with whatever you need, so if you need to work in the evenings, we can make that happen."

I give her an apologetic smile. "For now, I do. I can come over right after I finish with work."

She nods, and I gather my things in preparation to leave. Her brusque manner and tight-lipped answers leave me feeling unsettled, but I shake off my unease and try to focus on the task at hand. I'm excited to get back to my apartment and start my designs in earnest, now that I've seen the materials.

I spend the rest of the afternoon and into the evening working. By ten PM I have a finished sketch I'm proud of, and a thrill runs through me as I look it over. I'm itching to start working on a pattern, but that will have to wait.

The conversation with Logan from earlier drifts into my mind, and before I can overthink my decision, I send him a photo of the sketch.

TAYLOR

This is what I'm working on for Vince. What do you think?

I set my phone down to get ready for bed, and when I pick it back up after brushing my teeth, his response is waiting for me.

LOGAN

Whoa, that looks amazing! But I thought you didn't show other people your preliminary designs?

What made you change your mind?

I bite my lip, typing my response.

TAYLOR

I figured I owe you. For telling Vince about me
and giving me this opportunity.

He responds almost immediately.

LOGAN

You don't owe me anything, Taylor. That's
what friends do. I was happy it worked out.

I smile. It's going to take some getting used to, but so far it
feels pretty good—having my neighbor for a friend.

TAYLOR

Thanks. I'm glad we're friends.

LOGAN

Me too

Chapter 8

I get up early on Sunday for a sunrise yoga class. The air is brisk when I leave my apartment, and I shiver in my light jacket, my breath misting softly in the pre-dawn darkness. The yoga studio is only two blocks over, so I tuck my yoga mat under my arm and start walking.

"Taylor, you made it!" Cynthia calls as I pull open the studio door.

I smile at the instructor. "Finally, right? Sorry I haven't been by for a while—things have been busy at work."

"No apology necessary," she says. "You know you're always welcome, whenever you can make it."

I say hello to a few other yogis I recognize, then roll out my mat in an available space. Cynthia calls the class to order, and soon I'm stretching my mind and my body, letting my breath fill my lungs and expand my soul.

If you'd have told me ten years ago that I would come to love a morning yoga class, I'd have told you you were crazy. First of all, I was not a morning person then, and second of all, I was definitely *not* one of those granola-crunching, Chacowearing, basket-weaving hippies that I pictured whenever I heard the word *namaste*. Nope, not me. I'll take my Converse and tall double latte in a *disposable* cup, thank you very much.

But here I am at six a.m., eating my words.

It was my sister that got me into yoga, actually. After our dad died she went to therapy, and one of the suggestions of her therapist was to take up yoga. Being the supportive younger sister that I was, naturally I teased her about it, which meant that being the kind older sister *she* was, she dragged me to class with her.

The rest, as they say, is history.

Oh sure, I joked about it on the way to and from the studio each time, but it didn't take long for Rachel to realize that she wasn't the only one benefitting from all the slow breathing and conscious awareness exercises. My grades improved, my attitude improved, and my relationship with my sister improved. We grew closer, even as our mother grew more distant. And the way I came to see it, embracing yoga was a small price to pay for the relationship I now have with my sister.

As I walk out the door after class, I snap a quick selfie and send it to her.

TAYLOR

> Sunrise yoga! Can't wait till you move here and can do it with me 🧘

I send it off, wondering if she's already awake or if Marc is home and she can sleep in. Her reply comes a moment later, so I guess she's already up.

RACHEL

Good for you! I can't wait for that either

BTW, I think we may have found a house! 🏠

I start to reply as I walk home, but soon my phone vibrates and her face pops up on the screen. I laugh quietly. Rachel always prefers to talk instead of text.

"So you found a house?" I ask as I cross a quiet street.

"I think so. I hope so, anyways. We've only seen it online, since we don't really have time to make a house hunting trip. But the realtor we're working with is great, and has sent me all the photos and videos I've asked for."

"That's great," I say, as a random raindrop falls on my cheek. "Where is it?" I look up at the sky and get a fat, cold drop right in the corner of my eye.

"It's over in Randolph, New Jersey. Marc will have a bit of a commute, but I wanted some space."

"That's less than two hours from me," I say. "Although now that you're moving here, I might have to get myself a car. An Uber from here to there and back will bankrupt me in a week."

She laughs. "I'm sure you'll figure something out."

We chat the rest of the way home, but by the time I get to my apartment her kids are clamoring for attention and we say goodbye.

I take a quick shower and change into some comfy sweats, since I'll be spending the day inside instead of on the roof as planned. I don't mind, since I love my apartment. The space is small but well laid-out, and my minimalist aesthetic means it doesn't feel overly cluttered. My design table takes up one corner of the living room, a modeling dummy standing beside it near the window. Catalogues and fabric samples line the shelves beside the table, for once put away where they belong.

Pouring myself another cup of coffee, I curl up on the couch, watching the spring storm outside. The rain is soft but steady, running down the windows in haphazard rivulets. Twenty minutes later, I put my empty cup in the kitchen sink and sit down at my design table. Pulling out my laptop, I consult the email from Amelia with Vince's measurements. I sent my sketches to Vince last night, but with limited time available I don't want to wait to hear back before starting on the patterns.

The rain stops around six o'clock, right about the time my stomach tells me it's dinnertime. I stand and stretch before heading into the kitchen, but a glance in the fridge confirms that I haven't picked up any groceries for a while. Shoot. I'd rather not order takeout again.

Digging around in the freezer, I find a box of potstickers and a large lasagna, which reminds me of Logan. Grinning, I send him a quick text.

TAYLOR

> Want to come over for some frozen lasagna?
> There's no way I can eat it all myself.

I turn the oven on and pull it out of the package, then wash the few dishes in my sink. I make a quick sweep through my apartment to make sure it's presentable (ignoring my room, which is always a mess), and pop the lasagna in the oven. Logan hasn't replied, but I decide to go ahead and set two places at the table for us.

Ten minutes later I finally get a text.

LOGAN

Sorry, I'm going out with some friends
tonight. Want to join us?

I'm surprised at how disappointed I feel. Not disappointed
enough to suffer through small talk with strangers, but
disappointed enough to feel slightly pathetic.

TAYLOR

Thanks, but I'll pass. Have fun!

LOGAN

Can I take a rain check?

Glancing out at the gloomy drizzle, I allow myself a small
smile.

TAYLOR

Sure. The next time I raid my freezer I'll let
you know.

Slowly I put my phone down. The fact that I don't have
another friend to reach out to is an uncomfortable realization.
When did I become such a recluse?

*When your dad died? When your mom walked out? When
your college boyfriend cheated on you? Take your pick,* my brain
seems to say. In response, the walls around my heart tremble,
reminding me that it's easier, and safer, and less painful to keep
to myself. Best to focus on my career, and not on people who
will likely leave me.

Sighing, I put away the extra plate and utensils I had set
out for Logan. I guess I'll be eating leftover lasagna for lunch
the rest of the week.

———

I still haven't heard from Vince by the time I leave for work the next day, but I force myself to put it from my mind and focus on my day job. I'm not nervous, per se, but I'm hoping he'll give me the green light on the design so I can keep my appointment with Amelia on Tuesday.

The morning drags. I force myself *not* to compulsively check my email every hour, but it's hard. Then, just as I'm finishing lunch, he sends a reply.

Taylor,

You're brilliant! The designs are amazing, just as I knew they would be. And I love your interpretation of the Renaissance theme, especially with the ruffled back collar of the shirt. Can we make the shirt button all the way up the front and extend the ruffles all the way around the collar? I think it would be even more in line with the theme and would certainly turn some heads.

Vince

I read through his email twice, a sliver of unease worming its way into my gut. *It wouldn't turn them in the right direction, though* I think, chewing on my lower lip. Part of me wants to give in to his suggestion, just to stay in his good graces. Vince Milton is used to getting his way, and I'm not excited about the idea of shooting down his ideas on my very first job. But he *did* hire me to create a show-stopping ensemble for him, and I know that my design is perfect just the way it is. If I changed it to accommodate his wishes, it would ruin the whole aesthetic— and it would look ridiculous, too.

I spend the next half hour alternating between my own work at Totsworth and drafting a perfectly-worded response to my new boss. *Appeal to his ego,* I tell myself. *But stick to your guns—he wants you for a reason.* Finally satisfied, I send it off and get back to my work, forcing myself to let it rest.

His reply comes less than an hour later.

If you're sure, let's give it a shot. Send the design to Amelia so she can prep what you need, and let me know when you have it put together.

Relief courses through me, followed swiftly by a stab of panic. What if I can't deliver? What if he hates it? What if my vision comes out all wrong?

"Relax, Taylor," I tell myself. "It's going to be fine."

———

LOGAN

Sorry about the other night

I see Logan's text just before the end of the day on Tuesday.

TAYLOR

No problem. Did you have a good time with your friends?

LOGAN

Yeah, we had a great time. You should have come!

I don't respond, and after a few minutes he texts me again.

LOGAN

Want to grab some takeout tonight?

TAYLOR

Sorry, can't. Going to the studio after work to get started on the muslin.

LOGAN

I'm going to pretend I know what that means

I smirk as I type a response.

TAYLOR

It's like the prototype of the design. Meant to test out the pattern for fit and function before cutting up the nice fabric.

LOGAN

Ah, got it. And I assume muslin is a type of fabric that you use?

TAYLOR

Correct

LOGAN

So does that mean Vince liked your design ideas?

TAYLOR

Yup!

LOGAN

I knew he would

I smile, but just as I set my phone down he sends another message.

LOGAN

So no takeout tonight, but we're still on for the flower show on Sunday, right? I hope so, because I bought the tickets today

So much for buying my own ticket. I start to type "looking forward to it!" but I pause. *Sounds good* I type instead. Nodding to myself, I hit send and put my phone away.

I leave from work when I get the notification that my Uber has arrived, a few minutes before five o'clock. A buzz of excitement starts building inside me as we drive, like the hum of a crowd before the catwalk goes dark on a Tom Ford show. *I'm designing for Vince Milton* I tell myself, still trying to make it sink in.

It hasn't yet.

Amelia greets me at the door as I get out of the car. "You came," she says, as if surprised. I can see it's going to be an uphill battle to win her over. But I offer a smile and try not to let her see how nervous I am.

"I have a pattern ready—can you show me where the printer is?"

She nods and I follow her up the stairs. The printer is tucked in a corner out of the way, and I plug in my flash drive and pull up the pattern.

"We have a form tailored to Mr. Milton's measurements," Amelia says from behind me. "Will you need it tonight?"

"Yes, please, that would be great."

She nods and moves away as I wait for the machine to finish. Taking the freshly printed pattern with me, I head to the table Amelia showed me last time. Scissors, pins, and pattern weights are already laid out for me.

Amelia comes over with the dress form, then pulls a bolt of muslin from off the shelf and lays it down on the table.

"Would you like help cutting out the pattern?" she asks.

"It's fine, I don't want to bother you—"

Before I can finish the sentence she barks a command

across the room, and one of the seamstresses comes over. I rough cut around the pattern pieces, and the three of us lay them out against the fabric and begin cutting them out. When we finish, Amelia nods at me and the two women move on to their other duties. I breathe a sigh of relief when I find myself alone. She makes me nervous, and I don't want to mess this up.

I spend the next hour transferring the stitch lines and all the associated pattern marks to the fabric. It's been awhile since I worked on an adult-sized pattern, and the larger scale takes much longer to complete than I'm used to, but at last it's finished. The light outside has been fading while I worked, and as I stretch my back I notice it's almost completely dark.

"My team has left," I hear Amelia say, and I turn as she approaches the table, "but I can stay as late as you need."

I look over the table at the piles of paper and muslin and sigh. "I haven't got as far as I would have liked—do you mind if I stay another hour?"

She shrugs, but the motion seems less indifferent than it does judgmental. "Of course. Mr. Milton instructed that you are to have whatever you need."

"Thanks. If I can get the shirt and pants put together tonight, I'll come back to work on the jacket tomorrow. Would that be all right?"

"Of course," she says again. "Come, I'll show you which sewing machine you can use."

Chapter 9

I spend every evening for the rest of the week at the studio after work. I don't ever see Vince, or anyone else besides the seamstresses, and I wonder what the space is like during the daytime. Hopefully my position will become permanent and I'll get a chance to find out.

By Friday, the muslin is finally finished and fit to my satisfaction, and Amelia and her team take it in hand. They'll pull apart the pieces and use them as the final pattern with the official fabric next week, and once it's put together Vince will try it on. I feel nauseous just thinking about it, and I'm glad I'll have something to distract me this weekend.

"So what are you up to?" Rachel asks during a phone call on Saturday.

"Well, I finally finished the muslin for the design I created for Vince, so I won't have to go to the studio this weekend."

"That's great! Did it turn out the way you wanted?"

"I think so," I say, stretching out on the lawn furniture. It's the first time I've been up on the roof all week, and the sun feels good. "I can't wait to see it all put together next week, though."

"Are you nervous?"

"Of course I'm nervous! Wouldn't you be?"

"Not if I were you," she says. "You have the best eye for design of anyone I've ever seen, Taylor. It's going to be amazing."

Her words make me smile, and a lump of emotion fills my throat. "Thanks, Rach. That means a lot."

"You're welcome. I mean it, you know. I'm not just saying that."

"I know."

"So what are you doing to keep yourself distracted until then?" she asks. "Binging anything good?"

"No, actually. I'm going to a flower show with Logan tomorrow."

"Your neighbor?"

"Yeah. And coworker now, I guess. Although the position isn't permanent yet."

"Why are you going to a flower show with him?"

"Because he's really into flowers and plants, and he invited me to go with him," I say, feeling slightly exasperated.

"Since when do you care about flowers?"

I sigh. "I don't. It's a work thing, Rach."

"That doesn't sound like a work thing at all."

I bristle at the teasing tone in her voice. "It just so happens that the theme of the show this year is Flowers in Fashion, and they've teamed up with some local design students to help with the exhibit. So yes, it actually *is* a work thing."

There's a slight pause, and then Rachel asks, "So why didn't you say it was a work thing in the first place?"

I groan and cover my eyes, hearing her laugh. I can see her face in my mind as clearly as if she were standing in front of me: she's got one eyebrow lifted ever so slightly above the other, and her lips are pressed into a thin line, trying to hide a smile.

"Don't look like that, Rach. He's just my neighbor."

"How do you know how I'm looking, you can't even see me!"

I sit up on the lounger and cross my legs under me. "I know *exactly* how you're looking, Rach, but I'm telling you, it's nothing. He's just my neighbor."

"A neighbor who introduced you to Vince Milton? A neighbor you've had coffee with? A neighbor taking you to a *flower show*? That doesn't sound like any neighbor I've met, that sounds more like—"

"A friend," I cut her off. "Logan is my friend."

"And will I get to meet this *friend* in a couple months?"

I contemplate telling her no, but she would just take that as proof that Logan is more than a friend. Which he's not.

"Probably, unless he up and moves out of the building," I say instead.

"Mmm," she says, but this time I ignore the bait. The longer and harder I protest, the more convinced she'll be that Logan and I are a couple.

Which we aren't. At all.

———

Logan knocks on my door precisely at nine the next morning. The man is punctual, I'll give him that.

"Just a minute," I yell, fitting my final earring to my ear. Grabbing my purse and my keys, I pull open the door.

"'Morning, Taylor. Wow, you look great."

I glance down at myself. A cream blouse, black skinny jeans, and leopard print flats felt casual enough, but Logan's reaction makes me worry that I'm overdressed.

"Is it too much? Should I go change?" I ask.

"No, no, of course not. I just meant to give you a compliment," he says, rubbing the back of his neck self-consciously. "You ready to go?"

"Ready," I say, stepping out onto the landing and locking the door behind me.

We grab some coffee from the café and head to the nearest station. Despite my initial reluctance, I'm actually looking forward to the show. I've been meaning to check out the Botanical Gardens ever since I moved here, I've just never made the time.

It takes about an hour and a half to get to the gardens by train. As soon as we sit down, Logan sheepishly pulls out a book.

"Do you mind if I read on the ride there? Or would you rather talk?"

"I don't mind," I say.

He smiles his thanks and settles into his seat. Curious, I glance at the cover.

"*Pride and Prejudice?*" I ask, surprised.

"Yeah. Have you read it?"

I shake my head. "I'm not much for classic literature."

He turns the book over to look at the cover and shrugs. "Me neither. But a friend recommended it to me, so I said I'd read it. I was supposed to have it finished by now, so I'm trying to make up for lost time."

I don't know whether I'm more surprised that Logan is

reading a 19th century romance, or that he's reading it at the recommendation of a friend—a *female* friend, I'd suspect, because what man in his right mind would recommend reading *Pride and Prejudice* to another man?

While Logan reads, I scroll through the photos on my phone, deleting duplicates and organizing what's left. Pulling out my sketchbook, I draw up a few rough designs based on some of the photos I find.

"Did you get the... um... prototype-thingy for Vince finished?" Logan asks when we switch trains.

I grin. "The muslin."

"Yeah, that."

"I did. We'll see how the real thing looks on him sometime next week."

"Are you nervous?"

I nod, draining the last of my coffee. "Incredibly."

"You'll be fine," he says, bumping my shoulder with his own.

My sister said basically the same thing, but somehow it feels different coming from Logan. I don't know if it's what he said, how he said it, or the way he bumped my shoulder that sent a jolt through my middle, but it's a bit unsettling.

Flustered, I nod at the book he pulls out once again. "Is it any good?"

"Better than I expected, actually. Once you get past the archaic language, it's quite witty."

I raise my eyebrows. "Witty?" I say with a smirk.

"The language rubs off on you after a while."

I snort a laugh and turn back to my own work.

After a few transfers we finally make it to the botanical

gardens. A crowd of similar-minded New Yorkers move en masse toward the giant glass dome of the Haupt Conservatory, Logan and I in tow. He turns to me and waggles his eyebrows. "You ready for this?"

"Bring it on, Alexander."

He grins, opening the door for me.

A wall of warm, dense air slams into me as I step inside, so heavy with moisture I can practically drink it. As if the air wasn't enough of a surprise, the sheer amount of vegetation within has me hypnotized. An explosion of green surrounds us, speckled here and there with bursts of color, the trickling sound of water in the background making me feel as if I'm in the middle of the jungle. Ahead of us is a large water feature, dotted with mannequins wearing living clothing. Strings of globular leaves hang from one head like pearly hair, while another model features a crop top of lichen and moss.

"This is amazing," I murmur. Logan just grins at me.

We wander through the conservatory, stopping to inspect and photograph all the models and mannequins we see. It's not long until my interest is captured by the plants themselves.

"What is that smell?" I ask at one point, sniffing the air and looking around. "Is there a café in here?"

Logan indicates a cluster of flowers growing out of the trunk of a nearby tree. "You're probably smelling the Sharry Baby orchids over there."

As I draw near the small blossoms, the smell of chocolate becomes more pronounced. "That's coming from the *flowers*?" I ask.

He nods. "They call it the Chocolate Orchid, for obvious reasons."

I inhale slowly, and the rich fragrance fills my nostrils. There's a spicy undercurrent to its sweetness, hanging in the air and hovering in the back of my throat, like Mexican hot cocoa. "It's wonderful."

The blossoms are small and spiky, brick red with just a hint of cream on the bottommost petal. "And this is an orchid?"

"Yeah, most of the flowers in here are orchids."

"Even those?" I point across the way, to where a white flower bigger than my palm is growing out of a clump of enormous leaves.

"Yup."

"And do they really grow like this? Out of the middle of a tree trunk?" I wave my hand at the eye-level cluster of flowers in front of us.

"They do," Logan says, pushing his glasses up his nose. "Orchids are epiphytes, which means they need the tree for structural support but not food or nutrients. They collect all that from the air."

"That's crazy."

"Orchids are pretty cool," Logan says, as we move on to examine another species. "I've never tried to grow them, though."

"Why not? You seem to know your way around plants and flowers well enough."

"Too intimidating. They're tropical plants, after all. They need heat and humidity to thrive, and that's not something I can offer with any consistency."

"Sounds like you could use a greenhouse on the roof," I say with a smile.

He stops in the middle of the walkway. "That's not a bad idea."

I huff a laugh. "I was joking!"

He grins at me and starts walking again. "Still, it's something to look into."

I roll my eyes and follow him down the path.

We spend the rest of the morning and well into the afternoon exploring the exhibit. After several hours I sit down on a bench and pull out my sketchbook. "Do you mind if I hang out here for a while? I want to get some things down on paper while they're fresh in my mind."

"Sure. Is it all right if I keep wandering around? There's a *habenaria rhodocheila* around here somewhere that I'd like to see."

"If I knew what that was, I'd probably be impressed," I answer drily, "but since I don't, knock yourself out."

"You sure you don't mind?"

"I would certainly mind it more if you stood there staring at me while I sketch," I say, shooing him away. "Go find your habañera flower thing."

As Logan heads away, I start jotting down ideas and sketching out some rough designs. I pull up the photo app on my phone and scroll through until I stop at one of the first flowers we encountered: a stunning crimson orchid with delicate yellow edging. Glancing between the image on my phone and the paper in front of me, I draw out the dress I can see in my mind. A bodice emerges on the page, followed by a long, narrow skirt. I draw delicate ruffles along the hemline and cap sleeves, making note of the colors I would use, and wondering if I should design it with a belt or a colorblocked waist. I cock my head to the side, making adjustments and writing out notes. I didn't bring my pencils with me, so I'll have to color it in at home, but I like what I see.

It feels good to design something just for the thrill of it—just because I was inspired by something and felt the itch to create. The dress will likely never be made, but it makes me happy nonetheless. I smile, tucking the sketchbook away as I get to my feet, then head down the walkway in search of Logan.

Chapter 10

I spend nearly the entire trip back to Brooklyn sketching. I scroll through my photos, asking Logan for help identifying certain flowers and jotting down notes when something catches my fancy.

Almost a dozen blouses and as many dresses and pantsuits fill the pages of my notebook, half-formed and nebulous, but thrilling and full of potential all the same. I can't remember the last time so many ideas flowed so easily.

"Thanks for coming along with me, Taylor," Logan says as we walk back to our apartment building from the train station.

"Thanks for inviting me," I say. "I didn't really know what to expect, but it was amazing."

He grins. "I'm glad you had a good time."

"I really did," I say. "And it did wonders for my creativity. There was so much inspiration, and it was incredible to see all the depictions the design students created for the show."

We pass a little Thai restaurant, and Logan pauses. "You want to get something to eat? We skipped lunch, you know."

I hesitate, itching to keep working on my designs. "I think I'll pass. I want to get some color on these sketches, and besides, I've got leftovers."

He nods at the purse slung over my shoulder, where my sketchbook is. "Anything I might see in person, in the future?"

I shake my head. "Nah, none of it would work for Vince. I was just letting the muse have a little fun. It's mostly women's clothing; nothing that will ever be made."

"Not even for yourself?"

I shrug. "Not likely. But if I ever have a reason to make a *haute couture* dress, then maybe."

I wave goodbye as Logan heads into the restaurant, anxious to get home now. I jog up the stairs to my apartment and unlock the door, heading straight for my drafting table. I pull out my sketchbook and leaf through the pages, my eyes landing on the dress based off the Crimson Pride orchid. My fingers trace the pencilled lines, remembering the vivid hues and the velvety softness of the petals. Pulling out my pencils, I get to work.

It takes me half an hour to get the colors and shading just right, and my stomach is twisting painfully when I finally put my pencils down. I heat some leftover soup in the microwave and grab a mineral water from the fridge. Taking my dinner back to my design table, I admire the finished image while I sip my soup.

Logan's question flits into my mind, *Not even for yourself?* I let the possibility dangle there, shimmering like gold in my head. "I don't need a new dress," I finally say out loud. "There's absolutely no occasion to wear anything remotely like this." But still I sigh, wishing there was.

A sudden impulse seizes me, the desire to bring this

beautiful design to life overwhelming my good sense. Who cares if I don't have a reason to wear the dress? I didn't become a designer because I wanted to wear everything I make, I became a designer because I want to make whatever I dream up.

I nod to myself, deciding. I'll design the dress for myself. Who knows? Maybe working for Vince will grant me a coveted ticket to some A-list event I'd never get an invitation to otherwise. Excitement thrums through me, my mind rifling through a mental catalog of textures and hues in various types of fabric, waiting to land on the perfect combination.

Hmm. I glance at the sketch again, at the delicate ruffles along the hemline, remembering the stark contrast between the crimson and the creamy yellow petals. A silk velvet would be perfect for the main dress, perhaps in a lovely wine color—it will capture the look and feel of the petals perfectly. The contrasting frills would be best in a light, gauzy fabric, but not chiffon. Something less smooth, less perfect, to mimic the irregular edges. I'll have to think on it.

I spend the rest of the evening and most of the next working on the pattern. It's a blessed escape from the anxiety of waiting for the seamstresses to get Vince's outfit put together, since Totsworth doesn't fill every hour of the day. Amelia calls me on Tuesday, letting me know that the final fitting will be on Wednesday afternoon.

I take a half-day off and leave the office after lunch on Wednesday. *Breathe,* I remind myself. *You have nothing to worry about. Vince loved the design.* But the twisting in my gut doesn't seem to agree.

The murmur of many voices greets me when I arrive at the

studio. As I reach the top of the stairs, I see Vince standing on a dais in the open space between the two halves of the space, surrounded by a handful of people. Amelia and the other seamstresses I recognize, but there's also a man taking photos dodging around them, and seated across the room at a tall table is Logan. There's a laptop open in front of him, and he waves when I look over.

I guess Vince is capturing the fitting for additional content.

"There she is," he says when he sees me, his voice slick as an oil spill, "the most talented designer in New York."

I flush at his praise, my cheeks tight from the effort not to grin like a maniac. I nod at him. "It looks good. Nearly a perfect fit." I look to Amelia. "Well done."

I can't tell if she didn't hear my comment or if she's ignoring me on purpose, but I hope it's the former. The photographer turns and starts clicking away at me, but Vince calls him back.

"I don't want any shots of her, Paul—just focus on the details of the fitting. No faces, for anyone."

"Right-o, boss," the man replies. He flashes me a smile and a shrug, but is soon back to photographing Vince.

I glance at Amelia, wondering what to make of what Vince said to his photographer. But there's no evidence his words had any effect on her. She stands a few feet away with her arms folded across her chest, watching Vince with an impassive look.

Brushing it off, I walk around the small dais, looking Vince up and down with a critical eye. *Click, click, click*—the camera captures a closeup of my hand as I reach up and pinch a pleat on the back of his jacket. "Can you fold your arms, please?" I ask Vince, and he does. I shake my head.

"These pleats should be a bit tighter. Can I see the cuffs?" *Click, click.*

Vince holds out his arms, and I nod approvingly. "Good." My eyes drift to the high-backed, ruffled collar brushing the back of his head, and a little thrill shoots through me. It's always amazing seeing my designs on living, breathing beings. It's as if my dreams have come to life as well.

I step back with a final nod. "If we can just fix the pleats, you should be good."

Vince narrows his eyes the tiniest fraction. "Good? I didn't hire you to be good, Taylor. I hired you to be the *best*. It should be perfect, not—"

"It will be perfect," I cut in, feeling cold at his look. "I'm sure of it."

Click, click, click.

I'm glad the photographer isn't capturing my face, because it's probably white as a sheet. The tension hangs in the air for a fraction of a moment, then suddenly Vince gives me a dazzling smile, and I wonder if I only imagined the menace in his eyes. "Ah, Taylor," he croons. "I knew it would be." He lifts my hand and brushes a kiss along the back of my knuckles, adding even more to his likeness of a medieval lord than his ensemble already supplies.

Click, click.

Before I can take a breath, he turns to Amelia, who starts instructing one of the seamstresses in rapid-fire Spanish. I fall back as Amelia steps forward, marking and pinning the pleats where they need to be taken in. The photographer weaves his way in and around them all, the constant clicking of the camera a staccato in my ears. When she finishes, her assistants carefully remove the jacket and head to the machines. They work while Vince lounges in a chaise across the room, looking bored. It's as if I'm suddenly invisible, watching a behind-the-scenes reel of Day In The Life of a Designer. Only the designer is me.

Which is still hard to believe.

The photographer follows the seamstresses for a few shots at the machines, then crosses the room to the table where Logan is sitting. I slowly drift toward them, not really sure where I'm supposed to be (or not be) and wondering if this is what I can expect all his fittings to be like.

I hang back a bit, not wanting to interrupt their conversation, but when Logan sees me he waves me over.

"Paul, this is Taylor," Logan says. The photographer sticks out his hand and gives mine a firm shake. "She's Vince's new designer."

"Temporary," I amend.

"Ah, I wondered who the Irish beauty was I've caught glimpses of this past week," Paul says.

I flush. "You've seen me around?"

"Only in passing, love." He winks at me. "Sorry 'bout earlier. Vince didn't tell me beforehand he didn't want any headshots, although I would've assumed he'd make an exception for you." He gives me a cheeky grin, but Logan rolls his eyes.

"Alright, Casanova, that's enough," he says. Paul calls a cheery goodbye and takes off with his camera while Logan shakes his head.

"Don't mind Paul, he's the world's biggest flirt," he says. "How'd the fitting go?"

"Good, I guess. Not quite what I was expecting, though."

He gives me a commiserating smile. "Vince rarely is."

I nod. "So what are you working on?" I ask, anxious to get the focus off myself.

"Content. I usually work from home, but I heard about the fitting and wanted in on the action." He grins.

"Will it always be like this, then?"

He shrugs. "Maybe, maybe not. Today is a big deal because it's your first design, and it's for the Met Gala."

"So the photographer won't be dancing around us every time?"

He laughs. "Paul is as unpredictable as Vince, mostly because he's at his beck and call. Sometimes he's here, sometimes he's not. But I wouldn't worry about him."

"Easy for you to say," I mumble.

We finish the final fitting a short time later, and Logan and I walk home afterwards. He must be able to tell I'm not in the mood to talk because he doesn't say much—just walks beside me with his hands in his pockets, watching the sidewalk and the people around us. By the time we get to our building, my nerves have overridden my excitement.

"Vince is going to look amazing, Taylor," Logan says, breaking the silence as we reach the landing. "You should be—"

"Will you come watch it with me?" I blurt out.

His eyebrows shoot up in surprise. "The Gala?"

"Yeah. Next Monday. I was planning to watch it alone, but then I thought..." My voice trails off. Thought *what* exactly? Why on earth did I invite him? I shake my head, trying not to think about the desperate vulnerability eating me up inside.

"Sure," he says. "Although I have to confess, I've never been to a Met Gala watch party before. Do I need to rent a tux or something?"

I let out a nervous laugh, grateful for his humor. "My living room has a pretty relaxed dress code," I say. "Come as you are."

"Noted," he says. He gives me a genuine smile, the cleft in his chin standing out. "Thanks for the invite."

I nod, not knowing what else to say. He steps away to unlock his door, then waves before heading inside. I wave back, feeling the gentle stirring of long-dormant butterfly wings stretching and fluttering inside.

Chapter 11

L ogan knocks on my door at six o'clock sharp the
following Monday. I answer the door with a huge grin
on my face. "You're right on time," I say. "They just started the
livestream."

He holds up a plate of slightly-overdone cookies. "I come
bearing gifts."

"I thought you couldn't cook?" I say, taking the plate
from him.

"I can't. It's Pillsbury dough—I just burned them."

I chuckle and step back, letting him come in.

"Have you ever been to the Gala in person?" he asks,
following me into my tiny living room.

"No, it's incredibly exclusive. And I wouldn't have the cash
for a ticket anyway. But I watch it every year—it's one of my
favorite events."

I set the plate on the coffee table while Logan sits down on
the couch. "Any idea when Vince might show up?"

"No—but he likes to make an entrance, doesn't he? I bet he
gets there halfway through the livestream."

We settle in to watch the guests arrive. The Costume Institute Benefit is always a fun one. Most celebrity events are full of fancy dresses and tuxedos, but with a different theme every year, the attendees' outfits at the Met Gala are always more flamboyant.

"That guy looks like King Arthur," Logan says, grabbing a cookie.

"Oo, look at her hat! That's gorgeous," I say, pointing to one of the newly-arrived guests, whose ebony hair is looped and tucked in elaborate braids underneath a sapphire-colored hat. "I bet she's wearing Madeline Hayes—it looks like her style."

The screen cuts to another camera, and suddenly Vince steps out at the base of the stairs, smiling for the crowd.

"That's him! That's him!" I scream, bouncing on the couch and hitting Logan with a pillow.

Logan laughs. "I can see, Taylor, calm down."

"Calm down, are you kidding me?" I hit him harder with the pillow. "Vince Milton is wearing *my designs* to the Met Gala, and you expect me to be calm?" I face the television again just as my phone buzzes.

RACHEL

I saw Vince! OMG he looks amazing T!! 👑👑

I grin at Logan. "My sister saw Vince! She said he looks amazing."

"Listen, they're talking about him," he says.

I put my phone down and turn the volume up on the tv. Sure enough, the commentator announcing the new arrivals is talking about Vince.

"*And here he is, ladies and gentlemen, Emperor365 himself, Mr. Vince Milton. There was talk that he might not make it tonight, but I'm happy to see that was just a rumor. Look at him, he's stunning!"*

"That high collar with the ruffled back really pulls in the theme while staying modern and edgy," another announcer breaks in.

"I wouldn't have expected less," the first one responds.

My face hurts from smiling so big. The cameras move on to other guests, and a feeling of immense satisfaction settles around me. He'll be listed in Vogue as one of the best-dressed guests tonight, I'm absolutely sure of it, and my name will be right there beside his: designed by Taylor O'Neill.

Logan bumps his shoulder into mine. "How does it feel? Seeing your designs on a red carpet?"

"Surreal," I say, my eyes still glued to the television screen. "Completely surreal."

"I have a feeling it's only the beginning," he says.

I look over at him and smile. "You're the one who made all this possible, you know, and I'm really grateful."

He smiles and ducks his head. "I really didn't do much— just mentioned I knew a designer."

I nudge him with my elbow. "You know it was more than that."

He shrugs. "Your work speaks for itself."

I shake my head and turn back to the tv. "Talent still needs opportunity, Logan. And you gave me mine. So thanks."

"You're welcome," he says, reaching again for the plate he brought. "Cookie?"

I make some popcorn and we spend the next hour watching the gala guests arrive. My sister keeps texting me, but I only respond half the time. I don't want to be rude to Logan, so I only send quick replies in between our conversations. I can tell she's annoyed, because after a while she sends me the following text.

RACHEL

What's with you, T? Usually you're a chatterbox during the Gala

I see her message and bite my lip. If I tell her I'm watching the gala with Logan she'll just make more inferences, and I don't want anything to ruin this night.

TAYLOR

Sorry. I'm not paying much attention to my phone because I just don't want to miss anything, you know?

RACHEL

Should we do a call so we can just talk? That way you don't have to take your eyes off the screen.

Logan glances over at me and I give him an apologetic smile. "Sorry, it's my sister. We usually have a long-distance watch party together during the Met Gala."

"Oh—do you want me to leave, so you can chat with her instead?"

"Are you kidding? It's way more fun to watch with someone in person." I give him another smile—genuine, this time—and send a quick reply to my sister.

TAYLOR

Nah. Let's just talk tomorrow, k?

I put my phone on silent and set it facedown on the coffee table. "There," I say. "No more distractions."

The ensembles are stunning. Various celebrities are

outfitted in designers whose names and styles I recognize, and even though I'm not there in person, it feels as if I'm brushing shoulders with them.

I mention a few of the bigger names to Logan, but it's clear he's not as knowledgeable as he led me to believe before. "Hey, I work for Vince Milton and *he* knows all the names in fashion, so that's gotta count for something, right?" he argues when I call him out on it. I just roll my eyes and grin, turning back to the tv.

What Logan doesn't know about fashion moguls he makes up for in knowledge of Elizabethan playwrights—particularly The Bard. He starts casting the attendees as various characters in Shakespearean plays. He has vastly more knowledge on the subject than I do, and I struggle to make any connections beyond characters in *A Midsummer Night's Dream* or *Romeo and Juliet.*

"Oh, now see that woman in the black? With the short hair?" he says. "She's gotta be Lady Macbeth."

"Didn't she kill her husband?"

"No, she didn't kill anyone but herself. But she talked her husband into killing the king, so..."

"I knew there was a dead guy in there somewhere," I mumble. "What about him?" I say, pointing at a man in a green velvet suit. "He looks like he'd make a good Puck."

Logan rolls his eyes. "You've pointed out at least three other guys who would *also* make a good Puck. Is that the only play you know?"

I throw a handle of popcorn at him, and he laughs.

I can't remember the last time I had such a great night. We laugh, we talk, we snack, and when the guests have gone inside and the commentary ends, I don't want it to stop.

"Well, that's it, I guess," I say, turning off the tv.

"Wait, they don't film the actual gala?"

"Nope—there's a strict no phone and camera policy enforced inside."

"Oh. I didn't realize that."

"Yeah, it's kind of a bummer, but we can always check out the exhibit this summer and imagine what it's like there tonight."

"I'd like that," he says, returning my smile.

He starts cleaning up the popcorn while I take our dishes into the kitchen.

"Thanks so much for coming over, Logan," I say, when my living room has been returned to its clean, uncluttered origin.

"Anytime," he says. "It was fun."

I follow him to the door. "Congratulations, Taylor," he says, stepping out on the landing. "Vince looked amazing tonight."

A flicker of warmth fills my chest at his look, and the longer Logan smiles at me, the larger the flame grows. It fills me up completely, and I can't tell if it's pride in my accomplishment, or... something else.

Something about Logan.

"Thanks," I say, trying to douse the flame inside. It persists, like one of those trick candles on a birthday cake.

"Well, goodnight," he says.

"'Night."

I shut the door and lean back against the wood, my face pulling into a grin. My cheeks are sore and I'll probably have trouble sleeping tonight, but I don't care. Tonight has been the best night of my life, and if what Vince said at the restaurant is true, it really is only the beginning.

Chapter 12

I practically float to work the next day. Vogue's article was published in the wee hours of the morning, and just as I suspected, Vince made the best-dressed list. Words like "stunning," "trend-setting," and "fresh" accompanied the description of his ensemble, of *my design*. I finished the article feeling better than I did in third grade, when I won first place at the county fair for my homemade raincoat—like I can conquer the world.

The only thorn tempting to burst my bubble was not seeing my name listed as the designer in the article. Usually Vogue includes "model was wearing such-and-such designer" or "designed by so-and-so" in their descriptions. But there's nothing. Not a single mention of my name, or even that Vince is working with someone new. There's nothing about me on his social media accounts either, although I recognize some of the shots Paul took during the fitting. It's all a bit unusual, but not enough to really concern me. I assume it's because this was just a temporary gig, and Vince is waiting to announce me as his new designer until—and if—it becomes official.

My phone buzzes from its place on my desk as I'm going through my schedule for the week. When I see Vince Milton's name on the screen I nearly stop breathing, but I manage to answer the phone without passing out.

"This is Taylor O'Neill," I say, willing my voice not to shake.

"Taylor! It's Vince. Did you see the article?"

I glance around to make sure I'm alone. "I did, yes. Congratulations!"

"Oh thanks babe, I owe it all to you."

I flush, pleased at his praise. And he called me *babe!*

"Listen," he says, "you did such an amazing job and on such short notice, I can't wait to see what you can do with a few more weeks."

I suck in my breath. Is this it? The moment I've been waiting for?

"I'd like to bring you on full time, as my personal designer. Starting immediately."

He tells me what my salary will be and a few other details, but I hardly register the words. Vince Milton wants me—*me!*— to be his personal designer.

"So what do you say, Taylor—are you ready to make history with me?"

I'm about to tell him yes when that prickly little thorn from earlier pokes my side. I pause, letting the question that's been hovering in the back of my brain since I saw the article float to the surface.

"Vince, I'm honored. Truly. But I do have one question, if it's all right to ask?"

"Of course."

I take a steadying breath. "Is there a reason my name wasn't listed as the designer in the Vogue article?"

There's half a beat of silence, and then I hear his low chuckle.

"Taylor, my love, can't I keep you my little secret for a while? As soon as word gets out about you, you'll be beating off other clients with a stick, and I'd like to keep you all to myself for now. Surely you can understand that."

"Of course, I just wondered—"

"How about a little bonus for your trouble, hmm? Another ten grand to your salary, if you promise to keep our partnership under wraps for now?"

His words are like honey, sticky and sweet. But there's an undercurrent of menace in his voice, and the unease I feel threatens to choke me. I swallow it down, refusing to let go of this possibility

"Of course," I say again. "I'd be honored."

"Fabulous. I'll have my assistant send over the contract for you to sign, and let's chat about the Tony's soon. And remember Taylor—you're my little secret."

He ends the call and I stare at my phone, feeling equal parts elated and apprehensive. I shake off the dread before it can settle in my gut. *This is my chance.* If I ever want to see my designs on the runways of New York, Vince Milton is my ticket to get there. And if I have to keep my new job under wraps for a few weeks, who cares? Certainly not my bank account.

I sit back down at my desk, a bubble of excitement finally starting to build. The salary Vince mentioned is nearly double what I'm currently making, and since he wants me at his beck and call, it looks like I'll be quitting my job. I've never loved working for Totsworth & Company, but they've been good to me—I'll be sorry to say goodbye. Swallowing my guilt, I pull up an email and start typing.

Just as I finish, my phone rings. I glance at the screen, feeling a twinge of shame when I see my sister's face. I click *send* on the email and answer the phone.

"Hey, Rach."

"Hey yourself." There's a pause. "So what gives? Why did you ditch me last night?"

For one second, I contemplate lying to her. But I've never lied to her before, and she'd see right through me, anyway.

"Sorry, Rach. It wasn't that I didn't want to talk to you, I just... I was watching the gala with a friend."

There's another pause, and then she says, "Logan?"

Inwardly I bristle. "I have other friends, you know."

She laughs, short and hard. "Ha! Name one." When I don't respond, she sighs. "Why didn't you just tell me?"

"Because you seem to think that Logan is more than a friend, and I didn't want to deal with that again."

"Oh."

"Yeah."

Neither of us say anything for a while, and I wonder what she's thinking. Before I can ask, I hear her sigh. "I'm sorry. I know I shouldn't be teasing you about him, it's just... I don't know. You've been so serious and career-driven for so long, I haven't had much to tease you about."

"You don't have to tease me at all, you know."

"I know. But what's the fun in being a big sister if I can't tease you every now and then?"

I laugh quietly to myself. "Fair enough, I guess."

"I'll try to tone it down, though."

"Thanks."

With the air clear between us, my sister's voice takes on her usual cheer.

"So have you heard anything from Vince since last night?"

All my excitement from earlier comes rushing back to me. "I did—and he offered me the position!"

I pull the phone away from my ear as she screams, laughing. After a moment I put it back to my ear, grinning.

"Taylor that's incredible!" she says. "I'm so proud of you! And not at all surprised; he'd be an idiot to pass you by."

A notification pops up on my screen that I have a new email. "Thanks," I say, clicking on the notice. It's from Greg, and it's short.

Come see me in my office

"Have you told your boss yet?" Rachel asks.

"I just sent him an email, before you called."

"What do you think he'll say?"

"Well, he just replied that he wants to see me in his office, so I guess I'm about to find out."

"Oof. Well, good luck. Let me know how it goes."

"I will."

———

"You're leaving?" Greg looks incredulous.

I sent the email all of ten minutes ago, but here I am, standing in front of my boss. I sigh. "I am, yeah. Sorry."

"Is it about the pay? Can I make a counter offer? I'd really like you to stay, Taylor."

95

I smile. "Thanks, but it's not about the money. Just an opportunity I can't refuse."

He sighs. "Figures. The good ones always leave. As soon as I manage to sign on a promising new designer, some other company gets wind of them and off they go," he grumbles.

"What about Marjorie and Jason?" I quip, unable to stop myself. "They've been here for ages."

He waves a hand dismissively. "They're good, and they're consistent, but they can't do everything." He looks at me appraisingly. "So. Who snatched you up?"

I hesitate, remembering what Vince said. "It's a private label," I finally say, hoping that will satisfy Greg.

His eyebrows shoot up. "Oh hoho, heading out on your own, are you?"

"What? No!" I say, my voice sounding more defensive than I intend.

"Why not?" Greg sounds surprised at my denial. "You'd be great. Your designs are fresh and unique. You could really make a name for yourself."

I narrow my eyes and prop one hand on my hip. "It's funny to hear you say that, because you just shot down my latest collection for that very reason."

Greg leans over his desk, suddenly serious. "Some of your ideas aren't right for Totsworth, but that doesn't meant they aren't brilliant."

I blink. Did he really just say that? I stare at him, stunned.

He sits back. "I'm sorry to see you leave, but if you're determined to go, I wish you all the best."

"Th-thanks." I'm still reeling from his compliment. He thinks my designs are brilliant?

"Three days is hardly the standard two weeks' notice, but if there's ever anything I can do for you, just let me know. You'll always be welcome back at Totsworth."

"Thanks, Greg. I appreciate it."

I head back to my desk feeling strange. *Greg thinks I'm good enough to make a name for myself on my own?* The thought is both exhilarating and laughable. I've dreamed about it, of course, but in the same way first graders dream of going to the moon or becoming a dolphin trainer. Sure it's possible, but the chances are slim to none of it actually happening.

I shake it off, throwing an anchor to my aspirations and hauling them back to earth. I told Greg I'd work through Friday, and I have several things to wrap up before then. Pulling up the Vogue article on my phone, I download the image of Vince from the Gala and prop my phone up next to my computer screen. I grin.

I did that. Those are my designs. And they're going to carry my name all the way to Fashion Week someday.

Chapter 13

"Taylor! Vince told me the good news. Congratulations!" Logan says. He's standing out on our landing as I come up the stairs after work.

"Thanks!" I pause before the last stair. "Have you been out here, just waiting for me?"

A hint of pink creeps up his neck and into his ears. "No, actually. I, uh, saw you from the roof."

I chuckle, shaking my head. "Figures. What are you doing up there? Taking care of your flowers?"

The hint turns into a full-on flush. "No, just... hanging out."

I cock my head, giving him a questioning look. But he ignores me, clearing his throat instead. "So what's next?" he asks.

I let it go. Logan is entitled to his little secrets, after all.

"The Tony Awards. I have about a month to put something together, which should be cake after only having a couple weeks last time."

Logan grins. "You'll do great."

"Thanks." I reach to open my door, but then I pause. "You

want to grab something to eat? I'm famished and feel like celebrating. My treat."

"Taylor O'Neill, after all your refusals to have dinner with me, are *you* actually asking *me* out?"

A flutter of nerves balloons in my stomach at his smile, but I ignore it. "We're *friends*, Logan. This isn't a date. Besides," I say, tossing my head dramatically. "You're not my type."

He laughs. "Of course not. Your type would be tall, dark, and handsome, right?"

"Nope." I pop the *p*, unlocking my front door. "Short, blonde, and freckled, actually." I look down my nose at him. "And I don't see any freckles."

He laughs again, and I swing the door open wide for him. "Come on in. I gotta get out of these shoes."

He hesitates. "Actually, I left my things on the roof. I'll go grab them and meet you back here in ten minutes, okay?"

I narrow my eyes at him. "Logan Alexander, what are you doing up there? Should I be concerned?"

He laughs, but I can tell it's forced. "No, no, nothing to be concerned about. Just a little hobby of mine." He turns on his heel. "Be back in ten!"

"You better not be making a Chewbacca costume!" I yell, watching him head up the stairs. I wonder again what he's hiding. I'm not overly concerned about my neighbor being a serial killer or anything. Just... curious.

Heading into my apartment, I kick off my shoes and make my way to my bedroom. As orderly as I try to keep the rest of my apartment, my bedroom is anything but. The bedsheets and duvet are rumpled and unkempt, and half a dozen pairs of socks litter the floor. I'm pretty good about hanging my work clothes, since I *really* hate ironing, but yoga leggings and tshirts are another matter entirely. After pulling a tshirt from a pile of clean laundry in the corner, I grab a pair of jeans from a drawer and put them on.

A few minutes later Logan knocks on my door. "Mind if we order-in instead of go out? I'm feeling exceptionally lazy," I say, holding the door open for him.

"Not at all," he says. "Exceptionally lazy is my favorite state of mind."

I laugh and head for the kitchen. "Make yourself at home. I just have to finish emptying the dishwasher."

He wanders across the living room to my drafting table while I finish putting the plates and utensils away. "You want something to drink?" I call. "I've got iced tea, water, white wine..."

"Iced tea would be great, thanks."

I pour him a glass and walk over to hand it to him. He's leaning over my design table, staring at the sketch of my orchid dress.

"What's this?" he asks.

"Oh, that's just something I sketched after the flower show."

"It's beautiful."

I smile. "Thanks. I thought so, too. And you know what? I decided to take your advice and make it for myself."

His face lights up. "Really?"

"Really. I mean, I probably won't ever have a chance to wear it, but it's been fun to work on the pattern."

"Well, good for you. I can't wait to see it."

He takes his glass and follows me back to the kitchen. "I told my boss I'm leaving," I say, pulling a goblet out of the cupboard.

"How'd he take it?"

I shrug. "He was fine. Really understanding, actually."

"That's great."

"Yeah." I pull out an open bottle of wine from the fridge and pour myself a glass.

He raises an eyebrow. "But?"

I sigh. "But what if I'm not good enough? What if Vince hates what I do for the Tonys and he fires me?"

"Not possible."

"But—"

"Taylor," Logan says, his tone serious enough that I glance up to meet his eyes. "Your designs are amazing. Vince was right to snatch you up. I mean, you came up with that beautiful dress," he points toward my drafting table, "just from seeing a bunch of *flowers*. You're brilliant."

I give him a small smile. "That's what Greg said."

"Greg?"

"My boss. He said my designs were brilliant. He thought I was leaving to go it on my own." I take my glass and head into the living room. "You want pizza or Chinese?"

"Your boss said that?"

"Yeah. Shocking, right?"

But Logan shakes his head. "Not at all. Your designs *are* brilliant. Starting your own label isn't a bad idea, but... well, I hope you'll stick with Vince for a while."

"And why's that?"

"Well, you know..." He rubs the back of his neck, then lets out a small laugh. "If you start your own label, you're sure to become rich and famous, which means you'll move into some posh new condo in Manhattan and I'll have to endure a new neighbor—some old lady who probably smokes and owns a dozen cats."

I stifle a laugh. "A *dozen* cats?"

"The building will smell like a giant litter box, Taylor," he says, with an exaggerated sniff. "Do you really wish that for me?"

I smile. "Alright, I'll stick around for a while. For your sake."

His face splits into a giant grin, and my stomach swoops. I clear my throat, ignoring the fluttery feeling in my midsection. "So, pizza?"

We order a couple pies from our local wood-fired pizza parlor and settle down on the sofa to wait for delivery. Logan pulls out a pack of playing cards. "Fancy a game while we wait?"

We play Speed on the coffee table, slapping the deck and arguing over the rules when we tie. I haven't played a game in years, let alone a fast-paced card game, and I'm rusty. But soon my natural competitiveness wins over and I'm screaming and hollering, slapping the deck and whooping in delight when I win.

I don't know *what's* come over me.

The pizzas arrive in the middle of our fourth game. "Time!" Logan calls, when he hears the knock and I don't. *"Time!"*

"What? Oh," I say as Logan gets up to answer the door. He brings in the food and I take his drink to the table. My glass is empty, so I head into the kitchen to refill it.

"Are you sure you don't want any wine?" I ask, looking over at him and holding up the bottle. "I don't have any champagne, but we *are* supposed to be celebrating."

His smile is strained. "Thanks, but I don't drink."

"Oh, that's right." I pause while refilling my glass. "Do you mind if I ask you about that?"

"Not at all."

I turn to face him. "Is it that you used to drink and now you don't, or have you never had a drink?"

"The former." He clears his throat self-consciously. "I'm four years, seven months sober. It's not something I take lightly."

My body stills as his words sink in, an icy claw gripping my chest. "You're an alcoholic?" The words come out far more accusatory than I intended.

"Recovering." His smile is still strained, and his ears are definitely pink. "But yes. I was an alcoholic."

Without a word, I turn and empty my glass in the sink. Then I turn the bottle upside down and dump the contents down the drain. The *glug, glug* makes my stomach turn, but I don't stop.

"What are you doing?" Logan steps into the kitchen. "You don't have to do that, Taylor. It's fine."

"No, it's not. And yes I do." I watch the last of the wine trickle down the drain. I turn on the faucet and wash down every last drop. Then I rinse out the bottle and set it on the counter. I take a slow, deep breath, and finally look up at him.

"My dad was an alcoholic," I say quietly, folding my arms tightly across my middle, trying to thaw the ice inside, "before he died."

He watches me for a long time. "I'm sorry," he says at last.

I lift one shoulder. "It's okay—it was a long time ago. But I remember what he was like, every time he tried to quit. He'd be okay for awhile, and we thought maybe it would stick, but inevitably there'd be a party or celebration somewhere, and he would..." My voice trails off and I look down into the sink, where I dumped the bottle. Logan doesn't say anything, just watches me and waits. Finally I look up at him again.

"Even if you're not drinking it, being around someone who is can be pretty hellish, right?"

"Yeah."

"Well, there we go." I relax my arms, uncomfortable with the serious topic and anxious to end the conversation. "I couldn't do much for my dad—he died of alcohol poisoning—but I can help you out by not drinking when we're together."

I force my lips to smile, and slowly his face softens. "Thanks, Taylor. That means a lot."

An awkward silence follows, and in the quiet I feel a shift in our relationship. Not a major shift—just a subtle settling into solid friendship, one that's built not just on conversation and chemistry, but on action and behavior.

I pull another glass from the cupboard and pour myself some iced tea. "Should we eat, then? Or would you like the battle to continue? I was just getting warmed up."

He chuckles, holding up his hands in a show of surrender. "I think we'd best call a truce for the time being. I'm starving."

I grin. "Me too. Let's eat."

Chapter 14

O n my last day of work, Greg orders lunch for everyone. There's a giant cake in the breakroom, too, with "Good luck, Taylor!" written in green frosting across the top, with shamrocks dancing around it. If anyone is shocked by my sudden departure they don't show it, and I appreciate the well-wishes from my coworkers.

"It's going to be strange not having you here," the receptionist, Sam, says to me while sipping from a red Solo cup. "We were hired on at the same time, remember?"

"Oh that's right," I say, trying not to show that I actually *don't* remember this detail.

"So where are you going?" she asks.

"I'll be designing for a private label," I say with practiced ease, having answered a dozen variations of the question already this week.

"You're not running off to law school or something?"

"What? No, of course not," I laugh. "Where did that come from?"

She shrugs. "Just that it sounds like you don't want to say

where you'll be working. Everyone's talking about it, you know. Your answer is just so... secretive." Her eyes dart to the corner, and I follow her look. The Dream Team is chatting with Greg, his back to us.

I feel a flush of anger, but I tamp it down. "Let me guess: by 'everyone' you mean Marjorie and Jason, right?"

She grimaces and shrugs.

"I'm not surprised at their gossip," I say, trying not to let my irritation show. "But it's nothing like that. I'll definitely still be designing, but I'm not yet at liberty to say where. It's in my contract."

I give her a tight smile, and she returns it with a soft, apologetic one. "Well, good luck, Taylor. I'm sure you'll do great wherever you're going."

She walks off to get some cake, and for a moment I let myself seethe. So Marjorie and Jason think I'm quitting the profession, do they? Well, let them think that. They'll be greener than the frosting on the cake by the time word gets out that I'm working for Vince Milton, and then *I'll* be the one laughing.

The conversation with Sam leaves me deflated, and suddenly everyone's congratulations and well wishes feel half-hearted and fake. I leave the break room to go clean out my desk, wishing the day was already over.

Instead, I sit down in my chair and text my sister.

TAYLOR

> Marjorie and Jason are telling everyone that
> I've quit

When she doesn't respond right away, I start cleaning out my drawers. After ten minutes, she finally replies.

RACHEL

You did quit, didn't you?

TAYLOR

I mean they're telling people that I'm leaving the industry

RACHEL

What? Why?

TAYLOR

No idea

RACHEL

They're just jealous, T. Forget about them.

I sigh. I know she's right, but it still rankles.

RACHEL

Did I tell you the funny thing Grace said the other day?

TAYLOR

Tell me

RACHEL

We had gone to storytime at the library, and one of the songs the librarian sang with the kids was The Hokey Pokey. Grace LOVED it. So for days afterward, she would dance around the house singing the words she could remember.

TAYLOR

Too cute

RACHEL

That's not the funny thing. The funny thing is that she couldn't remember the name of the song, so when Marc asked her what she was doing, she told him she was dancing the Hoopie Doopie

107

The conversation with my sister calms me down a bit. By the time I leave at the end of the day, I'm genuinely sad to say goodbye to Greg, and even manage a smile for Marjorie. Jason doesn't bother coming out of his cubicle.

I take an Uber home after work, not wanting to carry my boxes on the train. But instead of putting everything away, I leave them on the floor and head to my bedroom. Talking with Rachel certainly helped, but the conversation in the break room brought back the unsettled feeling that came on the heels of the Vogue article. Anxious to shake it off, I slip into some workout clothes and head back out the door. A little evening yoga is sure to do the trick.

I take my thick mat up to the roof with me, remembering the rough, uneven surface and not wanting to subject my knees to that. Pushing open the door to the roof I look around. There's a canvas tote bag sitting near one of the lounge chairs that looks as if someone forgot it, and across the way I see Logan, watering his flowers.

"Hey, Logan," I call.

He looks over his shoulder, then turns around. "Taylor, hey! How's it going?"

"Alright," I say, setting my water bottle down on the low table and spreading out my mat in an open space near the lounge chairs.

"I haven't seen you much this week."

"I've been busy," I say. "I had to finish up my work at Totsworth. Today was my last day."

"You don't look too happy about it."

I shake my head, not wanting to get into it. "It's not that I'm not happy. There's just something else bothering me, and no, I don't want to talk about it," I say, giving him a pointed look.

He holds his arms up in mock surrender, his right hand still holding the red nozzle attached to the hose. I sigh.

"Sorry. I've just been on edge lately. Which is why I came up here—I wanted a little sunshine with my yoga tonight. Do you mind?"

"Not if you don't," he says, turning back to his flowers.

"Thanks."

Sitting cross-legged in the middle of my mat, I close my eyes and breathe in, letting the air expand my lungs and bringing my awareness into my body. I stretch my arms wide overhead, breathing in rhythm as I bend my upper body and stretch first one way, then another.

The sound of metal scraping along the flat roof draws my attention, and I open my eyes. Logan is pulling one of the low tables closer to his chair, a book on his lap. The canvas bag I saw earlier is sitting at his feet.

"What are you doing?" I ask.

He pauses. "Reading. Is that ok?"

"I thought you were just up here watering your flowers."

He shrugs. "That too, but I like to hang out up here when I can. Since I work in my apartment all day I get a little stir crazy inside. But seriously, don't mind me." He lifts his book in a salute and settles back into his chair.

I let out a small laugh. "Yoga isn't really a spectator sport, you know."

"I'm not spectating, I'm reading," he says, though I can tell he's watching me over the top of the page. I roll my eyes.

"Whatever," I say, getting to my knees and trying to ignore

him as I reach into a warrior two pose. I steady my breathing, focusing on stretching the muscles in my arms and back, willing the tension to leave. I blow out my breath and close my eyes, bending into downward dog. When I open my eyes again, Logan is watching me.

"You look as if you've never seen someone do yoga before," I say.

"I haven't. Well, I mean... I have, like on tv and stuff. But never in person. It's... different."

"In what way?" I get down into a side plank, opening my arm wide and stretching up to the sky.

"I don't know." He shrugs. "I just thought it was about incense and meditation and contorting your body into weird positions. But this is... not that."

I glance at his face, but he's buried behind his book now, and all I can see are the tips of his pink ears. Sighing, I kneel down on the mat, scooting to one end and facing the other. "Come here, Logan," I say.

He looks up. "Pardon?"

I snort a laugh, recognizing the book. "Still reading *Pride and Prejudice?*"

He glances at the cover, then back at me. "Yeah? So?"

I shake my head. "Never mind. C'mere."

He unfolds himself from the chair and walks over to me. I pat the other end of the yoga mat, indicating that he should sit, which he does.

"Yoga is not about incense and contortion," I say, "and depending on your definition of the word, it's not really about meditation, either." I take a deep breath in, swinging my arms up over my head, then pushing out my breath as I let them swing back down. "It's about bringing your awareness into your body. About recognizing and focusing on the air moving in and out of your lungs, of the pull and release of your muscles. It's bringing your mind into harmony with your body, instead of letting your thoughts dictate what your body does."

He looks at me blankly.

"Here," I say, moving to sit cross-legged and resting my hands gently on my knees. "Follow me."

He arranges his body into a mirror of my own. I close my eyes, and I assume he does the same.

"Relax your shoulders," I say, "and pay attention to your breath. Notice how much or how little your chest expands. Notice the rhythm of your breathing. Try to synchronize the breaths, so you're breathing in for the same amount of time you're breathing out. Now notice the muscles along your jaw and neck and down your back. Focus on the ones that feel tight, and try to relax them."

I open my eyes to watch him follow my directions, but *he's* watching *me* with a grin.

"What?" I say, feeling strangely vulnerable.

"This is totally meditation."

I roll my eyes. "Fine, it's meditation. Whatever. Just do what I said."

"You know, I've never really been into all this woowoo stuff."

"*Woowoo* stuff?"

"Yeah, like we're all connected to this—"

"Logan."

"—Chi energy or something, and I—"

"LOGAN."

He stops, half a grin plastered on his face, his eyebrows

raised expectantly. His look stings, and I get to my feet, looking down at him.

"I don't know what exactly you mean by *woowoo* stuff," I say, crossing my arms, "but yoga isn't some sissy, hippy sport. It takes focus and dedication, strength and determination."

I pause, hearing the words I've spoken out loud like an echo from the past. In them I can hear my sister's voice, defensive and angry in response to my own mocking words.

Logan isn't smiling anymore. He, at least, seems to be feeling some remorse already, which makes him a far quicker study than I was—I tormented my sister for weeks before I finally caved.

My cheeks flush with regret.

"Listen," I say, sitting back down.

"Taylor, I—"

I hold up a hand, cutting him off. "Just listen, please?" He nods, and I continue. "I know how you feel. Ten years ago, when my sister started doing yoga, I felt exactly the same way. And I teased her constantly about it." I pause, looking down at the mat.

"She started yoga at the suggestion of her therapist, after our dad died," I say. "It was a much healthier way to cope than I found."

I press a fingernail gently into the foam mat and watch it spring back, a tiny crescent indent marking the spot. I rub it with my finger.

"What did you find to help you cope?" Logan asks, his voice gentle.

I shrug. "Angry music. Boys. I tried some things—weed and stuff—but it made me sick so I didn't do it again. I let my grades plummet, when before I was a dedicated student. I was just angry and hated everything."

He nods slowly, and I look back down, taking a deep breath. "When I finally realized how much my words and attitude were hurting my sister, I felt terrible. So I agreed to go with her, as a penance, sort of. To show that I was sorry and wouldn't do it again. I didn't expect to connect with it like I did. Like I do."

Logan doesn't say anything for a long time. The sounds of the city drift lazily around us, hardly noticeable for how familiar they are. A faint siren wails in the distance, and somewhere in the park, a bird cries.

"When I quit drinking," he says at last, "I had to find something, too. Something healthier. Some way to cope with the shame and the guilt and the cravings, the constant fight going on inside me."

I glance up at him. "Your plants?"

He shrugs. "Among other things."

"What things?"

A flash of something akin to panic crosses his face, but the next moment it's gone. "It doesn't matter. What matters is that I understand. And I'm sorry."

I nod, grateful for his apology. He sits up straighter, resting his hands on his knees and looking at me with a hesitant smile. "Now, can you walk me through that again?"

Chapter 15

Vince and I chat on the phone about the Tony Awards the next day. It's a black tie affair and there's not a lot of wiggle room for men's fashion, but he insists that he stand out in the crowd.

"Neon is all the rage this year," he tells me. "I want a fluorescent suit."

"Neon *is* very in this year," I hedge, "but it's better as an accent. Too much is overwhelming. What do you think about a fluorescent tie and shoes?"

"Along with the suit? That sounds fabulous."

"No, *instead* of the suit," I say, alarmed. "Neon is like a garnish—a little goes a long way."

"I want a fluorescent suit."

"I understand," I say slowly, trying not to panic, "but I'm afraid that a full fluorescent suit will be too much. It goes beyond being bold and borders on foolish."

"You know that *you* work for *me*, right babe?" he says, a hard edge to his voice.

"Yes sir," I say, careful with my tone, "but you hired me

because you said my designs were brilliant and you wanted *me* to design for *you*. If you let me do my job properly, I promise, you'll turn heads in only the best way."

I hold my breath, wondering if I've overstepped and will end up fired before I've even truly begun. But after a moment I hear his breathy laugh, and I release a silent sigh of relief.

"Taylor, no one has ever dared stand up to me like that, which means you're either confident or crazy. Let's hope it's the former."

I don't know what to say to that, but when he doesn't offer any more instruction, I clear my throat. "So... neon shoes and tie instead of a suit?"

"If that's what you think is best," he says. "Send me a sketch as soon as you've pulled something together."

I hang up the phone and sag in relief. Logan wasn't kidding when he said Vince was a diva, but I wasn't expecting him to be so... well, diva-ish. It's certainly going to make my job harder if he's questioning every decision I make.

I make some notes and do a bit of research, but then I close my laptop and get up off the couch. I wander over to my design table, looking at the sketches strewn there and thinking about my orchid dress. I started working on a pattern a while ago, but I haven't finished it yet. Since I don't need it for anything, I just keep shuffling it to the side, telling myself I'll get to it later. I think about working on it now, but the sun is shining and the air holds a hint of summer —it seems a shame to waste the day inside.

I've been spending a lot of time on the roof lately, so today I decide to head to the park across the street for some open air yoga. After changing my clothes, I grab a mat and water bottle and head out the door.

When I was looking for someplace to live, one of the biggest draws of this apartment is that it's right next to Fort Greene park. The park is old, with lots of grass and large, established trees, making it the perfect place when I need a change of scene and a breath of fresher air. I meander through the park, finally settling down underneath a beautiful maple tree.

I'm holding a crow pose when the vibration of my phone breaks my concentration. Unfolding myself, I reach for my phone and see Logan's name lit up on the screen.

"Hey Logan," I say, answering the phone. "What's up?"

"Save me, please. I'm begging you."

"Save you? From what?" I ask, brushing off a piece of grass stuck to my arm.

"My mother."

I laugh at his tone. "Your mother? I thought she lived in California."

"She does. But apparently she's in town, and she wants to come for dinner tomorrow night."

"What's she in town for?"

"A friend's birthday weekend, so thankfully I only have to manage her for one night."

I chuckle. "Is she really that bad?"

"Bad? No, my mom is great. She's just..." His voice trails off, and I picture him in my mind. He probably removed his glasses and is polishing them on his shirt. I've noticed that's something he does sometimes, when he's searching for the right thing to say.

"Concerned," he says at last.

"Concerned?"

"Yeah. About me. She thinks I'm lonely."

I frown slightly. "*Are* you lonely?"

"Of course not! I have friends. Besides, Yoda keeps me company."

I was taking a drink from my water bottle and nearly choke. "Yoda?" I manage to sputter. "Who's Yoda?"

"My goldfish."

"Your *goldfish* keeps you company?"

He chuckles. "Not really. He's just a fish, you know? But at least it's something to interact with every day."

"So your mom thinks you're lonely, even though you've got Yoda for company." I can't help the grin that stretches across my face as I say that. "You know how that sounds, right? That you have a goldfish to keep you company?"

"That's not the point. The point is that no amount of reasoning will get her to accept that I'm *not* lonely. So basically she wants to meet me for dinner to fuss over how thin I am and how neglected I look, and lament over the fact that I don't even have a roommate to make sure I stay alive."

"Because your roommate is a goldfish."

I hear him chuckle and it sends a little thrill down my spine. I grin in response.

"So, where do I come into all this?" I ask.

"Well, I was thinking... if you joined us for dinner, that would show her that she doesn't have to worry so much, you know?"

As his words sink in, a funny feeling fills my head, like breathing in helium from a balloon. "So, what... you want me to pretend to be your girlfriend?"

"What? No! Nothing like that. Just come and be yourself. Show her that I have friends. A neighbor who cares."

I silently breathe a sigh of relief. Logan is great and all, but

I'm not sure he's boyfriend material—even if it's just fake boyfriend material. And who said I'm girlfriend material? According to my Life Plan™, that's still something I don't have time for.

"So you want me to come have dinner with you and your mom, as your friend?"

"Yes, please."

I can't help the wicked grin that creeps onto my face. "What about the other Taylor? Is she busy?"

I'm not sure if he'll remember the joke, but he doesn't even miss a beat. "She's got a beard-growing competition. I called her first."

A laugh bursts out of me, startling a nearby squirrel. "Of course she does," I say, still chuckling.

"I have some other friends I can ask if you'd rather not," he says. "It's just that... well, you were the first to come to mind."

His words fill me with warmth, like a long drink of hot tea. "Alright," I say, "I'm in. What time is dinner?"

————

It's been another beautiful day, so the text from Logan the next afternoon telling me we'll be eating on the roof doesn't come as a surprise. Dinner is at seven, so at ten till I check my appearance in the mirror, grab a bottle from the fridge, and head upstairs.

The short stairwell between the fifth floor and the rooftop is sweltering, and I suck in a full, refreshing breath when I come out on top of the building. I see the same elderly woman tending to the vegetables that I've seen before, but no one else is on the roof. A small table is laid out with a tablecloth and place settings for three though, so I'm sure Logan and his mom will be up shortly.

Sure enough, just as I take a seat on one of the nearby lounge chairs, the door to the stairwell opens. Logan is carrying a covered casserole dish while a middle-aged woman (his mom, I assume) carries a salad bowl.

"Taylor!" Logan says, his face splitting into a grin. "Glad you could make it." He sets the dish on the table and removes the mismatched oven mitts from his hands.

I join them and hold out the bottle I brought. "Thanks for inviting me. This is for you—well, for us. I thought we could have it with dinner. It's sparkling cider," I say quickly, noticing the look of concern on his mother's face.

Logan's eyes brighten with a smile. "Thanks, Taylor. It sounds delicious." His mom sets the bowl of salad on the table. "Mom, this is my friend and neighbor, Taylor O'Neill. Taylor, this is my mother, Virginia Alexander."

"Just call me Ginny," his mom says, shaking my hand. Her accent isn't as strong as I expected—just a hint of Southern twang, soft and light, like sweet tea. She smiles at me warmly. "Logan has told me so much about you."

I laugh lightly. "I doubt there was much to tell—I lead a pretty boring life."

"Not from what I hear," she says as we all take our seats. "You're a fashion designer, aren't you?"

"Yes, but—"

"No buts about it, sweetie, that's mighty interesting." She smiles, and I notice that she has the same cleft in her chin as Logan.

"Well, should we eat?" he asks. "Nothing fancy—just spaghetti and meatballs."

"I'm impressed, Logan. I was half expecting Stouffer's lasagna," I tease, dishing some salad onto my plate.

"Don't be too impressed; all I did was cook the noodles. Everything else was store bought," he says with a laugh. His mom huffs.

"Logan, don't tell her that—how do you expect to win her over if you tell her all your secrets?"

Logan's ears turn pink. "I'm not trying to win over Taylor, Mom. We're just friends. And it's not like it's a secret that I can't cook."

"But you said—"

"So Taylor," Logan cuts in loudly, "have you seen any good shows lately?"

I cough to hide my laugh. "Um, not really, no. I don't watch much television."

"I'm a crime show fanatic myself," his mom says. "I've always liked mysteries, and trying to figure out whodunit before the other characters do is such a thrill."

"What about you, Logan?" I say, twisting together a forkful of spaghetti on my plate. "I know you're a Star Wars junkie—what do you think of the new spin-off shows?"

Logan looks surprised. "I thought you weren't a fan?"

I shrug. "I'm not, really. But I know enough about the franchise to hold my own in a conversation."

He laughs. "If I had known that, I'd have talked your ear off about them before now."

The food is good, despite Logan's lack of culinary skill. He obviously picked quality premade stuff, but whether it was for my benefit or his mother's, I'm not sure.

"So what sort of hobbies do you have, Taylor?" Logan's

mom asks. "Are any of those grow boxes yours?" she says, indicating the vegetable garden on the other side of the roof.

I glance over my shoulder, but the geriatric gardener is nowhere in sight. "No, I don't know a thing about plants. I had a fern once, but it died."

"You should get a snake plant," she says matter-of-factly, stabbing a meatball. "They're impossible to kill."

I meet Logan's eyes across the table, but quickly look away, stifling a laugh. He looks as amused as I am.

"Do you have any pets?" she asks.

"No."

"Do you like to read?"

"Not really."

"Any artistic pursuits you fancy?" she persists.

I shake my head. "I don't have much time for hobbies, to be honest. I live and breathe my work, pretty much."

"You don't have any hobbies at all?" She looks as shocked as she sounds.

I lift a shoulder and smile. "I enjoy yoga, but I love my work so much, I don't ever feel like taking a break from it, really."

"You don't read or play an instrument or paint or *anything?*"

"Mom, not everyone has hobbies," Logan says, frowning at her.

"Of course they do!" she huffs. "Everyone has hobbies. And if they don't, they should. It isn't healthy not to have a life outside of work."

Her words strike a nerve, and I frown, feeling defensive. "The fashion industry is my life. And I enjoy it."

"Honey, it's great to love your work, but you need

something to *do!* Logan," she says abruptly, laying a hand on his arm, "you should teach her how to knit."

I nearly choke on the sip of cider I just took, my defensiveness melting away. Logan's face turns as red as the sauce on his plate.

"Mom, I..." His eyes dart to mine, a look of pure terror in his eyes. "She doesn't... I haven't..."

"You knit?" I say, incredulous.

"Oh honey, he's wonderful," his mother goes on, either not noticing or not caring about her son's embarrassment. "He made me the most lovely sweater for Christmas last year, didn't you, sweetie?"

Logan looks as if he'd like to disappear. He keeps his eyes glued to his plate, his face now a brilliant shade of red. My heart goes out to him, and while my natural inclination is to tease him about this "other hobby" of his, I decide to be kind.

"Knitting and crocheting have always intimidated me," I say, keeping my voice level. "I can turn fabric into clothing, but creating clothing straight from yarn or string? That takes some serious talent."

Logan's eyes flick to my face, his pained expression softening slightly. I give him a brief smile, hoping he knows it's genuine and not mocking.

"Well, I'm sure Logan could teach you, couldn't you, Logan?" His mom doesn't wait for a reply. "He picked it up in detention his junior year of high school. The librarian taught him."

"All right, that's enough," Logan says abruptly, tossing his napkin onto the table. "Mother, *please.* This is exactly why I haven't invited friends to join us for dinner in the past. Is there anything else you'd like to bring up, besides my juvenile delinquency and secret hobbies?"

"Secret! What do you mean, secret?" Her voice pitches in concern. "Why do you keep your knitting a secret? You are *very* talented and it's nothing to be ashamed of!"

"Most men my age don't knit," Logan mumbles, stuffing a meatball into his mouth.

"Well, most men your age..." she huffs, looking towards me. I feel my cheeks warm, and I drop my gaze.

She doesn't finish the thought.

The rest of the meal is subdued, and Logan's mom maintains a rather offended silence. Logan hides his embarrassment under a façade of polite inquiries about my family and past work, more for his mother's benefit than his own, I'm sure. I keep my conversation equally polite and neutral, following his lead.

We don't linger after the meal. Logan's mom appears to be thawing out, but he obviously doesn't want to encourage any more familiarity between her and I. He starts tidying up as soon as we're all finished eating.

"Thanks for dinner," I say, helping him stack the plates. "Can I help take things down?"

"Sure, that'd be great."

I grab the salad and follow him down the stairwell. His mom has her arms folded across her chest and is staring off into the distance, so I assume she'll wait up here for us to return.

We walk in silence back to his apartment, but when we reach his kitchen he heaves a sigh. "Sorry about my mom," he says. "I should have known she'd..." He shakes his head.

"No problem," I say. "And hey—no worries. Your secret is safe with me."

I give him a smile and drag my finger over my heart in a cross shape. He blushes, but at least he laughs a little.

"Well, seeing as how you're the only person I cared about keeping my knitting a secret from, it doesn't matter. But I appreciate the sentiment."

"Me? Why?"

He shrugs. "It's no Comic Con obsession, but it's not exactly what you'd call a 'manly' activity, you know?"

I move the stack of plates he set on the counter into the sink and start washing them. "Who cares? If it's something you enjoy, does it matter?"

My back is to him so I can't see his face, but after a moment he comes to my side and starts drying the dishes. "I guess not." He clears his throat. "Do *you* think it matters?"

I rinse the last plate and hand it to him with a smirk. "Does what I think matter?" Before he can answer I continue. "Knitting is cool. Although I'm curious what landed you in detention."

He groans, and I laugh. "I'm never inviting friends to dinner with my mom again," he says, shaking his head.

He doesn't say anything else as he puts the salad in a container and pops it in the fridge. My curiosity gets the better of me, and I bump his shoulder on the way back upstairs.

"Are you ever going to tell me?"

He stops. I worry that he might be angry or embarrassed at my question, but there's a sparkle in his eye as he turns to look at me.

"What do *you* think I was in for?"

I narrow my eyes, looking him up and down. "Hmm. From what I know about you, I'm going to guess... lost library items."

He snorts a laugh. *"That's* what you think, from what you know about me?"

"Sure. A highly intelligent, gentleman-like young man who's—admittedly—a bit awkward and nerdy?"

"You forgot my most important characteristic."

"What, your charm?"

His smile is surprised. "You think I'm charming?"

That crooked little cleft in his chin pops out, and my eyes trace his jawline. "No, I just..." I shake my head, distracted. "What characteristic?"

"I'm an I.T. guy, remember?"

"Oh, right. So what, you got caught playing games on your phone during class?"

"Nah." He starts up the stairs again, and I follow. "I hacked into the school computer system to try and change the grades in one of my classes."

"Wait, what?" I grab his arm to stop him. "Are you serious?"

He laughs sheepishly, looking away. "Yeah. I got caught before I was able to do anything, though. I was lucky to get a month of detention instead of being suspended or expelled, you know?"

I shake my head, a slow grin spreading across my face. "Logan, you are *way* cooler than I ever gave you credit for."

He laughs, obviously relieved at my reaction, as we head back up to the roof.

Chapter 16

A few nights later I dream about Logan.

It's one of those weird, nebulous dreams that drift from place to place and person to person, and I lie in bed thinking about it the next morning. I was wandering through the city looking for him, feeling anxious, and I felt so relieved when I finally found him. He laughed at my worry and took me to the café to get some coffee. But then suddenly he was my dad drinking a beer, and I was crying and telling him to stop but he just laughed and kept drinking until I ran away.

I decide to ignore whatever my psyche is trying to tell me, and don't mention it to Rachel when she calls me an hour later.

"So the sellers accepted your offer? That's great, Rach!" I put her on speaker and set my phone down so I can flip my omelet before it burns.

"Thanks. It's not quite as big as we were hoping for, but the schools are supposed to be good, and it's only an hour commute for Marc."

"When can you move in?"

"We asked for a fast closing, so it should be in the next few weeks. Are you still going to come help us get settled?"

"Absolutely. Just tell me when and where and I'll be there."

I turn the omelet one last time to check the other side before lifting it onto a plate.

"Great. You should bring your neighbor, too."

I pause. "Logan? Why?"

"Why? Because I want to meet the guy my sister is dating, that's why."

I nearly drop the plate. "We are *not* dating, Rachel. We haven't even been on *a* date."

She scoffs into the phone. "Oh come on, Taylor, you like the guy!"

"Of course I like him. We're friends."

"You know that's not what I meant."

I set my plate on the table and turn back to get a fork. "Oh I know what you meant, but whether I like him or not doesn't even matter, because we're *just friends*."

"Mmhmm."

I roll my eyes, even though I know she can't see me. "Why are you so convinced there's something more going on?"

"Because you talk about him constantly—"

"I do not!"

"—you're spending all your time with the guy—"

"We work together now, you know."

"—and you haven't had a date in what, three years?"

I take a bite of my omelet, and my sister lets the silence hang between us. I deliberately take my time chewing before swallowing.

"You're being ridiculous," I finally say.

"*You're* being ridiculous, Taylor," she says, but her voice is softer. "Why are you so scared to let someone in?"

"I'm *not* scared. I just..." I sigh. Logan's face drifts across my mind, his surprised smile bringing out the cleft in his chin. My stomach flips at the image, but suddenly his face morphs into that of my father, like in my dream. I squeeze my eyes shut, trying to block out the sight.

"Taylor?"

Rachel's voice seems to come from far away. I blink.

"I'm here," I say quietly.

"Are you okay? You got really quiet all of a sudden, and I—"

"He's an alcoholic," I blurt out, and the line goes silent. I start counting, more to stop the onslaught of painful memories than because I'm waiting for something. It takes seven seconds for my sister to respond.

"Logan is?"

"Yes. He's a recovering alcoholic."

Two more seconds.

"How do you know?"

"He told me himself, the day Vince offered me the job. He came over to celebrate with me. I offered him some wine, and when he told me he doesn't drink I asked him about it. He said he hasn't had a drink in over four years."

"Oh, T," she says, her soft voice is laced with understanding. "That must have been a shock."

I blow out my breath in a long exhale. "Yeah."

"But it sounds like he's *actually* sober, you know? Not like Dad. Dad never made it more than a month. Four years is a long time."

"I guess, yeah." I take another bite of breakfast, but the eggs feel like rubber in my mouth. My stomach turns.

"I just don't think I could ever be with someone like that," I say, getting up from the table and dumping my plate in the sink.

"Like Dad? Taylor, Logan doesn't sound *anything* like him."

"You don't know that, you haven't even met the guy," I say, but my voice sounds weak, even to my ears, and my hands are trembling.

"Look, Taylor," Rachel says, pulling out her no-nonsense, big-sister voice. "You can't shut people out just because you've been hurt before. I know it's scary, and I know how hard it can be to let someone into your heart again. But you deserve better than a lonely, painful, celibate existence."

My lips twitch. "Celibate?"

"You know what I mean. You deserve to be loved and adored by a man, and to love and adore him in return. And if Logan's not the guy, well, there will be someone else someday. But you have to let yourself try, Taylor. You have to believe there are good people in the world who aren't going to leave you all alone."

I close my eyes and take a shaky breath. "Are you finished?"

Three seconds.

"Yeah, I'm finished."

"Good."

She doesn't hang up, and neither do I. I pile the rest of the dishes in the sink and put away the eggs and cheese. Wetting a rag, I wipe down the stove and the counters, then take it down the hall and drop it in the washing machine. I can hear Rachel on the other end of the line, murmuring something to my niece that I can't quite make out. I feel equal parts dismayed and relieved by the sound. I hate that I'm taking her away from her kids, but I'm glad she's staying with me.

She's always stayed with me.

The tension fades away as the silence between us grows. It's a comfortable silence, and I'm grateful for the time and space it allows me to sort through my emotions. After ten minutes she asks if I'll be going to the yoga studio today.

"Maybe later," I say. "I've been working on a pattern for a dress and I'd like to finish that up today."

"A dress? For who?"

"For me. It's a formal design, so it's not like I'll have any occasion to wear it, but it's been nice to do something just for fun."

"Good for you. I can't wait to see it." She pauses. "Are you going to be okay?"

I blow out my breath, running a hand through my tangled curls. "Yeah, I'll be okay. I just didn't expect to get into all that today, you know?"

"Yeah, I know. I'm sorry."

"It's all right. I'm glad I told you. And I'm glad you were here for me."

"Always." She pauses. "Marc is calling on the other line. Chat later?"

"Sure."

"'K, love you."

"Love you too."

———

I'm so exhausted after talking with my sister that I go back to bed. I wake up two hours later feeling *much* better, ready to give the day another chance. After a quick shower, I start a load of laundry and then sit down at my computer. The pattern for my dress is almost complete, and within an hour I have it finished. Saving it to a flash drive, I drop it in my purse and head to the studio.

When I signed the contract with Vince, I was given a key so I could work whenever I needed to. Amelia and I have a polite working relationship now, and although she is helpful and accommodating, she keeps me at arm's length. I can't say I blame her—my contract included a gag clause as well. And even though I know I have as much right to the studio as anyone else, I still feel like I'm trespassing in Amelia's domain every time I'm in here. Unlocking the door, I head up the stairs, hearing the now-familiar thrum of the sewing machines before anything else.

Huh. That's odd. The team isn't usually here on Saturdays.

I shrug off the anomaly and continue up the stairs. If Amelia is here, it will give me a chance to ask her something I thought would have to wait until Monday.

I felt unsettled after talking with Vince a few days ago, about his attire for the Tony Awards. I knew I was right—a full fluorescent suit is WAY too much, but my initial idea of just a neon tic and shoes started to feel flat. Vince wants to stand out in a fluorescent suit, and while I'm not *that* crazy, the idea of a classic pinstripe, with fluorescent thread woven into the stripes, started to take shape in my mind. It was intriguing, and the longer I thought on it, the more I liked the idea.

I sent my sketch of the neon-striped suit to Vince last night, and he responded almost immediately that he loved it and couldn't wait to see it pulled together. His enthusiasm gave me a welcome boost of confidence, because I know it will be expensive to have a bolt of fabric custom woven for the suit. But

Logan has insisted that money isn't an object, so it's time to test that theory.

Taking my sketch and measurements in hand, I go in search of Amelia. I find her speaking to one of the seamstresses by the machines. At my approach, they both stop talking and Amelia turns toward me. The other woman scurries away.

"Yes?" she asks with her usual briskness.

"I was wondering how I go about ordering custom fabric."

I'm prepared to show her my design and argue my case, expecting her to resist the expense. But she merely turns and heads toward her small office in the corner. I trail behind, assuming she meant for me to follow. Pulling out a large binder from one of her shelves, she hands it to me.

"All of our suppliers are listed in here," she says. "Most of them can provide custom fabric upon request. Once you've decided where you want to order, simply call or email them with what you need."

"That's it?" I ask. "You don't need to approve the purchase or anything?"

She shrugs. "You are the designer. You get to decide what we create."

She turns and walks away, and as I watch her go I realize that Amelia is not the one in charge around here, *I* am.

Feeling both giddy and terrified at the thought, I set the book down on my table and start leafing through the pages. It's going to take a while for the fabric to be created and shipped, and I don't have any time to waste.

Chapter 17

The next few weeks pass quickly. I finish the muslin for Vince's suit and print off the pattern for my dress. Logan and I get together for coffee and takeout a few times, but he's busy the night of the Tony Awards and I end up watching them alone.

Vince's ensemble is a hit, as I knew it would be. He makes the best-dressed list again and gains several thousand more social media followers. His phone calls, emails, and texts to me are oozing with praise, calling me "babe" and "genius" and "the next big name in fashion." That last one is stretching it a bit, but I must admit to being flattered.

Perhaps *too* flattered.

Vince doesn't seem to recall his bad ideas at all, and never thanks me for saving him from himself —plus, he still isn't crediting me as his designer. The little voice in the back of my head insists on waving a red flag every time I notice these things, but I deliberately ignore her.

With the Tony Awards over and Fashion Week still months away, Vince won't need another designer ensemble for a while.

It's nice to have a bit of a breather, and I decide to take advantage of the break by visiting the Renaissance exhibit. The Met Gala kicks off the show each year, and I try to go every summer. I consider waiting until August to see if my sister can go with me, but I doubt she'll have the time, and I'm not sure I'll have another opportunity before it ends.

The next afternoon I take myself across the landing and knock on Logan's door. I can hear music coming from inside, and when he doesn't answer the door even after the second time I knock, I decide to text him.

TAYLOR

Knock, knock neighbor

A few seconds later I get a reply.

LOGAN

Hey! What's up?

TAYLOR

Your music is really loud. Would you mind turning it down?

Almost immediately the music behind the door disappears, and I grin.

TAYLOR

Thanks

I knock on the door again, and Logan opens it a moment later.

"Taylor!" he says, pushing his glasses back into place. "I am so sorry, I had no idea you'd be able to hear that from your place. I didn't think it was that loud."

I chuckle. "I couldn't hear it from my apartment—you just couldn't hear me knocking otherwise."

"Oh!" He tips his head back with a groan. "Geez, Taylor, I thought for sure you were upset because it was too loud, and then you'd never agree to—"

He stops abruptly. Clearing his throat, he runs a hand up through his hair, making it stand on end. "Anyways, sorry about that. Did you need something?"

"Yeah, I wanted to ask if you want to go to The Met with me tomorrow?"

He looks taken aback. "Do I want to go out with you tomorrow?"

"Well, not like... not *out* with me. Just... to go with me to the exhibit at The Met. You know, since we watched the Gala together, I thought it might be fun to go see the show together, too," I finish lamely, trying to ignore the bubbles ballooning inside.

"Oh."

We stand there awkwardly for a moment, before he runs his hand up through his hair again. "Sorry, Taylor, but I can't."

"Oh. Okay." The bubbles inside suddenly deflate.

"I really wish I could, but I'm actually heading to California tomorrow. I go every year at the end of June for a week, to visit my mom. I know she was just here, but I already had the ticket, so, you know..." His voice trails off, and he gives me an apologetic smile.

"No problem," I say.

"I'd really love to go, though," he says. "We could have cast all of *King Lear*."

I laugh lightly. "You would have had to cast it all by yourself, since I don't know the play at all."

"Well, I wouldn't have minded."

He gives me a crooked smile, and my stomach dips. "Maybe another time, then," I say. "Have a nice trip."

"I will, thanks."

He stands there watching me, until I turn and go back into my apartment, wondering why I feel so disappointed.

———

I end up going to the exhibition by myself. I always love to see the items on display each year, but as I wander through the exhibit I can't help thinking of Logan and how much fun we would have had viewing it together.

The last week in June passes far more slowly than I thought possible. Between waiting for my sister to move and Logan being out of town, the only thing motivating me from day to day is my work. Vince continues to throw terrible ideas at me, insisting they'll compliment my own style. I balk and cringe at the idea of putting my name to some of his more hideous suggestions. The worst to date? An electric blue, faux-fur vest in which the hair is long and matted into dreadlocks.

He insists it's art. I insist it's revolting.

"Like wearing a Muppet skin," I mutter, staring in horror at some similar fashion *faux pas* I've found images of online.

"Yikes. Please tell me you're not doing something like that for Vince."

I turn at the sound of Logan's voice, my lips curling up at the sight of him. I'm sitting at an outdoor table at the café down the street, but Logan seems to have seen me as he was walking past.

"Logan! When did you get home?"

"Just last night. How've you been?"

I gesture to the screen of my laptop and shrug. "Oh, just great. Josh Pratt is getting married next month—do you think this would be appropriate for the wedding?"

"Josh Pratt, the actor?"

I nod.

Logan's horrified grimace lasts only a moment before I laugh. "I'm kidding, Logan, geez. Have you so little faith in me?"

He breathes an exaggerated sigh of relief and sits down across the table from me. "You had me going there for a second, Taylor. You ever consider a career in acting?"

"No, but Vince should." I wave my hand at the screen again. "He's got a corner on clown costumes."

"*Vince* wants that?"

I nod, grimly.

He grimaces. "I'll say it again—yikes."

"You're telling me," I mumble. I pull the lid shut on my laptop and smile at him. "So how was California?"

He shrugs. "Do you remember the dinner we shared with my mom on the roof?"

I nod.

"Imagine a week's worth of that."

"Oof," I say, making a face. "Sorry about that."

"It's fine. At least I don't have to endure it for another year." He smiles, and I smile back.

"So are you heading home?" I ask.

"No, actually, I have a meeting." He takes off his glasses, cleaning them on the hem of his shirt. "I'm heading to my knitting club," he says, not looking up. "There's a group of us that get together once a month and hang out while we knit."

I can hear an edge of defensiveness hiding in his tone, but I know he's just embarrassed.

I give him a genuine smile. "Cool. What are you working on?"

He shrugs and gets to his feet. "I always have a few projects in the works. Do you... do you want to come with me?"

My eyebrows lift. "Like, right now?"

"Sure. Unless you have something else you need to do?"

"Not really. But I don't know..." I can't tell if the swirling in my stomach is excitement or nerves, and the feeling unsettles me. "I don't knit, and I've never really been much into crafts."

"Knitting is *not* crafting," Logan says. "Besides, I let you teach me some yoga." He strikes a pose (not a yoga one) and I laugh.

"Okay, fine," I say. "I'll come."

Chapter 18

The only solid memory I have of any of my grandparents is one of sitting on my grandma's lap and wondering who this strange woman was who looked vaguely like my father. She smelled strongly of cigarette smoke and laughed a little too loudly, but she gave me a piece of gum, so I sat there quietly while she talked to my mom and dad. That's the only time I ever recall meeting her, and I don't ever remember meeting my mom's parents. Their families just weren't very close, I guess.

I'm not sure what Logan's experience has been with his own grandparents, but when we arrive at the community center on Myrtle Ave, it's clear he has an army of grandmothers now.

"Logan!" one old lady croons as we walk into the room. "I was wondering where you were."

"Hi Cordelia," Logan greets her. "Everyone, this is my neighbor, Taylor."

I wave at the group, and another elderly woman—this one

with wavy, turquoise hair—nudges the tiny Asian grandmother sitting next to her.

"Is that his girlfriend? I thought you said he was gay?"

I glance at Logan with raised brow, but to my surprise, he chuckles and shakes his head.

"He's not gay, Madge," a well-dressed man sitting to my left says, getting up from his seat. He rolls his eyes but approaches me with a smile. "Hi Taylor, I'm Jonathan," he says, shaking my hand.

"And you would know," the little Asian woman says, pointing a knitting needle at him. Everyone chuckles at this, including Jonathan.

Logan nods at the two women who started the conversation. "Those two troublemakers," he says with fondness, and they giggle, "are Madge and Fumie."

"Nice to meet you, honey," the blue-haired Madge says, nodding at me.

Logan points to the only other people in the small group who haven't spoken yet. "And this is Sarah and her daughter Afton." The middle-aged mom and her teenager wave at me.

"Hi everyone," I say.

"Do you knit, Taylor?" Cordelia asks. She has a puff of white hair and such a soft voice, I'm surprised I can hear it at all.

"No, but Logan asked me to come, so I agreed to tag along."

"Come sit by us," Fumie says, patting the small stretch of fabric between her and her partner in crime. "Madge, move over, your butt is taking up the whole couch."

Logan quickly steers me to an empty chair next to Jonathan. "We're going to sit over here today, Fumie. Thanks, though."

We sit down and Logan pulls out some yarn and a couple of wooden knitting needles. "That was close," he mutters. "Who knows what they would have weaseled out of you?" He hands me the supplies with a grin. "Ready to learn how to knit?"

"You didn't say I had to learn how to knit," I argue. "I just agreed to come with you. Can't I just watch?"

"It's fun," Jonathan pipes up. "And not as difficult as it looks." He nods at Logan. "Logan here is a great teacher. He's the one who got me started, and now look what I can do."

He holds up a small purple sweater. At least, I think it's a sweater—the proportions seem too small, and the armholes are in awkward places, but I can't imagine what else it could be. As if sensing my confusion, Jonathan smiles.

"It's a dog sweater. Or it will be, when I'm done with it." He lowers it to his lap and starts working again.

"Jonathan loves dogs, so he knits little sweaters to donate to the Humane Society," Logan explains, pulling out his own knitting supplies.

I'm low key starting to panic at this point, because I never had any intention of learning how to knit. "Logan, I really don't know about this," I say again.

"You'll be fine," he says, giving me an encouraging smile. "Now, the first thing you need to know is that there are two basic types of stitches: the knit and the purl. But before we get to that, you need to learn how to cast on."

"You're speaking another language, Logan."

He chuckles. "Here, I'll get you started."

He takes the items back from me, pulls out a length of yarn, and drapes it over a needle. I try to follow the complicated pull-twist-loop thing he does with his hands, but I'm completely lost. Soon he hands it all back to me: one needle completely empty, the other with smooth knots of yarn tied in a neat line along the length of it.

"Okay, so put the needle with the yarn in your left hand, and hold the empty needle in your right. The empty needle is called your working needle or working hand."

I nod, and he indicates the supplies in his lap. "Let me get to the same point and we'll go from there."

I watch him quietly, marveling at the happiness he exudes while he works. It's practically rolling off him as he twists and loops and pulls the yarn into position.

"You love knitting," I say.

He looks up at me, his eyebrows slightly lifted. "I do, yeah."

"I mean, you *really* love it. Like the way I love designing clothes. I can tell."

His looks softens, and a feel a hitch in my chest. "There's something really therapeutic about it," he says. "Something about starting from a ball of yarn and two short sticks, and ending up with something beautiful. It just feeds my soul, you know?"

He's so earnest, and so endearing, that for half a second I wonder if maybe I *should* make room in my spreadsheet for a relationship. But I shove it aside and instead offer him a smile.

"I do know," I say, nudging his shoulder with my own. "I just said that."

He chuckles. "Yeah, I guess you did." He holds up his own needle and yarn. "So, you ready to get started?"

I nod, and the lesson begins.

―――

I've been knitting—slowly—for ten minutes, not paying much attention to the others' conversations as I concentrate on what Logan taught me. *Under the stitch, wrap it around, pull it through, slide it off.* Slowly, slowly a short length of knit yarn is emerging from the bottom of my needle. I have no idea if it looks the way it's supposed to, but at least it's progress. *Under the stitch, wrap it around, pull it through, slide it off.*

Jonathan's voice suddenly interrupts my mental chant. "Does anyone know where Lynette is today?"

The Grannies™ immediately start speculating, but it's the middle-aged mom Sarah who speaks up with any degree of certainty.

"I think she had to meet with the florist or the caterer or something," she says, her hands still working. "She said last month that she'd be late because of it."

Under the stitch, wrap it around...

"Oh, that's right," Cordelia says in her cotton-candy voice. "I forgot it's getting so close."

Pull it through, slide it off.

Nods and murmurs intermingle with the soft *tick-clack* of knitting needles. I lean toward Logan.

"What's getting close?" I say, trying to keep my voice down.

But The Grannies™ hear my question and pipe up before he can respond. "Lynette's getting *married*," Fumie says, clucking her tongue. "For the *second time*."

"Who cares how many times she's been married, Fu? Besides," Madge throws me a wicked grin. "I don't blame her. Dr. Hendelson is a hottie."

A laugh bursts out of me, echoed by laughs from the others. Fumie says something in another language and smacks Madge on the arm, and the two of them start arguing. Cordelia looks like she's hiding a smile, and Sarah shakes her head, grinning.

"She's not wrong," Jonathan says with a grin. "I could eat him up myself."

"There is no denying that Dr. Hendelson is handsome," Cordelia says, and everyone quiets in order to hear her. "And it doesn't matter that Lynette has been married before," she adds, giving Fumie a significant look. "What matters is that Lynette has found love, and we are all very happy for her."

Most of the others nod and murmur in agreement, but Fumie continues to mutter quietly to herself.

Another few rows later, a windswept woman with salt-and-pepper hair opens the door and strides into the room. "Sorry I'm late, everyone," she says, her heels clicking softly across the linoleum floor. "You would not *believe* the traffic on Atlantic Avenue. It was a *nightmare.*"

She parks herself in an empty chair next to Sarah, thrusts her hand into her bag and pulls out a slim black case. Snapping it open, she places a pair of glasses on her face, adjusts them for a moment, and stops, staring at me.

"Who are you?" she demands.

"Oh," I say, feeling like a cornered mouse. "I'm Taylor. Logan brought me."

Her eyes flick to Logan's face, and I follow her line of sight. Logan's neck is red, but he's smiling. "This is my friend, Taylor. Taylor, this is Lynette."

"So this is Taylor?" Lynette asks, her eyes darting back to mine. I don't miss the subtle emphasis she put on the word *this.* What has Logan told them?

"I'm his neighbor," I say, meeting her gaze and forcing my lips to smile.

"Lynette, how are the wedding plans coming?" Cordelia's voice floats over to us, and Lynette looks her way.

"Fine, fine," she says, her hands busily situating the knitting project that has appeared in her lap. "I met with the caterer again today and finalized the menu. Jeremy doesn't think we need the vegan option, but I was adamant, and in the end he agreed." The needles in her hands begin to flash and click with effortless precision.

"As if he'd dare to do otherwise," Madge mutters to her seatmate, who nods.

"You two better be on your best behavior at the wedding," Lynette says, glaring at them over the top of her glasses. "Just because Cordelia puts up with you *here* doesn't mean I'll put up with you *there*."

Madge gives Lynette a mock salute, and soon she and Fumie start gossiping about something else. I continue to work at a painstakingly slow pace. *Under the stitch, wrap it around, pull it through, slide it off.* The length barely grows with each added row, and if I wasn't switching needles and hands each time, I'd wonder if I was actually making any progress. Logan said it will be a scarf eventually, but I'm not sure it will ever get to that point.

Logan. I glance over to where he's chatting with Cordelia, who just called him over for some reason or other. He's listening to her with a smile on his face, giving her his full attention. Just like he listened to me when we first met.

"He's a really great guy, you know."

Startled, I look around. Jonathan is looking pointedly in my direction. "What?"

He gives me a knowing smile, nodding his head toward Logan. "You heard me."

"He is, yeah," I say, looking back down at my project in an effort to hide the warmth I can feel creeping up my neck.

"He started this knitting club, you know," Jonathan says. "And he does a lot of work to keep it going."

"He *started* the club? I thought—I mean, I just assumed that Cordelia is in charge."

"Well, she *is* kind of the mother hen to us all. But Logan is the reason we started getting together. It was about... hm, let me see... four or five years ago? He found each of us on his own and brought us all together."

Logan's voice drifts into my mind. *Four years, seven months sober.*

This was how he coped, I realize, the pieces clicking into place in my mind. "Huh," I murmur, glancing back at Logan. "He started a knitting club. Go figure."

I hear Jonathan chuckle beside me, and I turn back toward him. "How did you guys meet?"

He gives me a wry smile. "Don't listen to Fumie, he's not gay. We actually ran into each other getting coffee one day. I complimented him on his scarf, he told me he made it himself, and the rest, as they say, is history." He nods at Lynette, who's deep in conversation with Sarah about something. "He met Lynette when he accidentally took her luggage at the airport, thinking it was his own. She gave him an earful, from what I hear."

I laugh quietly to myself. "I can imagine. She doesn't seem like someone you'd want to cross. But somehow he managed to turn her into a friend."

"Yup. He's made friends out of all of us, and now we're all friends because of him. He's the glue that keeps us all together."

Logan is now helping the teenager, Afton, with something. I watch as he refers to something in the book on her lap, then takes up the needles and demonstrates for her. I smile.

"He really is a great guy," Jonathan says again, and I realize he's watching me. I quickly turn my attention back to my work.

"He's a good neighbor, too," I say without looking up.

"Is he *just* your neighbor?"

"Well, he's my friend, of course. But that's all."

Jonathan doesn't look convinced. He opens his mouth, closes it, and returns to his knitting. I'm too afraid to ask what he was going to say, so I let it go. I wonder again what Logan has said about me here, but I try to focus instead on the wannabe scarf hanging off my needles. When I'm sure Jonathan is focused on his work, I sneak another glance at Logan. He's still sitting next to Afton, but I catch him looking at me this time. His face immediately splits into a grin, and I can't help but smile back. That kind of happy is contagious, even from here.

But when Logan turns to respond to another question from the teen, my smile fades. I turn back to my knitting and try to ignore the thoughts swirling in my head. *Under the stitch...* he's just a friend. *Wrap it around...* and he's known that all along. *Pull it through...* he's fine just being friends. Just being neighbors. *Slide it off.*

Isn't he?

Chapter 19

L ogan stops by the studio the next day as I'm putting together some wardrobe staples for Vince. "Hey," I call in greeting, looking up from the table where I'm pinning pieces of muslin together. "I didn't expect to see you here today."

"I wanted to stop by and say thanks again for coming to my knitting club with me," he says. "It was fun having you there."

I carefully avoid looking at him as I respond. "It was fun to be there, which surprised me. Everyone was really nice."

He doesn't respond, and I finally look up at him. "Was that it, then? You just wanted to say thanks?"

He smirks. "Well that, and make sure you didn't change your mind about the muppet suit," he teases. I glare at him, and he chuckles. "Actually," he says, "I wanted to ask you something."

The way he says it makes my stomach turn a funny flip, and I avoid the urge to glance over my shoulder at where Amelia and her team are working. "Sure, what's up?"

"Would you be my plus one at Lynette's wedding?"

I don't know what I was expecting him to ask, but it certainly wasn't that. "Lynette from your knitting club?"

"Yeah." He bends over, leaning his elbows on the table. "She's the one who came in late."

"I remember who she is," I say, turning back to my work. Jonathan's question from yesterday comes to mind. "As friends? Not like a date?" I ask

Logan rolls his eyes. "I think I've learned by now that nothing is ever a date with you, Taylor. So yes, as friends."

"Just checking," I say, wondering why his easy dismissal leaves me feeling slightly annoyed.

"There is one catch," he says.

"Oh?"

"It's a black tie affair."

I finish pinning the pieces of fabric together and look up at him with a grin. "You? In a suit?"

"I clean up pretty nice, you know."

I chuckle. "I'm sure you do."

"So what do you say?" he asks, "Will you come?"

"Of course. I can—" A flash of inspiration hits me, and I gasp. "The orchid dress!"

Logan's eyebrows shoot up. "Is that the dress I saw a sketch of on your table?"

"Yes!" I say as giddy excitement courses through me. "But I haven't even started on the muslin, even though I printed the pattern out weeks ago. How long until the wedding?"

"It's at the end of the month. July 29th."

"That shouldn't be a problem, as long as I order the fabric right away," I murmur to myself, doing some quick calculating. It will be tight, but I think I can do it.

"So you'll wear it to the wedding?" Logan asks, sounding as excited as I am.

"If I can manage to finish in time."

He makes an exasperated noise. "If you can put together a whole ensemble for Vince in two weeks, making a dress in a month should be a piece of cake."

"Easy for you to say!" I retort with a laugh. "But I'll order the fabric today." Suddenly I wish I could put Vince's work aside and start on my dress instead. But that would be irresponsible, and like Logan said, I've got time. Gathering up the pieces of fabric sitting on the table, I jerk my head in the direction of the sewing machines. "I have to get this muslin put together. Are you sticking around?"

"Nah, but there is one more thing." His mouth pulls up in a half-smile, hinting at a dimple in his cheek I haven't noticed before. He comes around the table to stand next to me while my heart knocks against my ribs.

He reaches his hand up toward my cheek and I take a slow, shaky breath, my eyes widening slightly.

"You have a thread in your hair."

I exhale in a puff as he pulls the string of cotton out of my unruly curls.

"Oh. Thanks," I say, trying to recover from... what, exactly? What *was* that? Expectation? Anticipation? Clearly I need to get my head checked.

"No problem," he says. Then, shoving his hands in his pockets, he rocks back on his heels. "So I'll see you later? You want to get some pho tonight?"

"No, I think I'll work on my dress after this, so I'll be staying late," I say, suddenly embarrassed and angry and irrational. I smile tightly at him and hurry off. "See ya."

I don't bother looking back to see if he heard me, just head to my sewing machine and plop the pile of fabric down. Sitting in the chair, I close my eyes and take a slow breath, forcing the fluttering in my belly to subside as I refocus my thoughts. Right now at this moment, I'm working for Vince. That's all I need to worry about.

After a minute I open my eyes, then grab a piece of the muslin and start feeding it through the machine.

I stay late at the studio—much later than I usually do. If I'm being totally honest, I'm afraid to go home and run into Logan. I'm afraid of what he might say or do, or what *I* might say or do if I see him before I can sort out the confusing jumble of thoughts and feelings tumbling around inside of me. Working on my orchid dress has been a good distraction. I've cut out the pattern and all the muslin pieces, but my own dress form is back at my apartment, so there's not much else I can do. Finally, at 2am, I decide to call it a night. I contemplate crashing on one of the sofas, but that would lead to awkward questions in the morning.

I put a call in for a taxi and pull up my favorite fabric distributor's website. While I wait for the car, I order the silk velvet I've been eyeing before I lose my nerve. Hopefully by the time Lynette's wedding rolls around, I'll have sorted out what's going on with Logan, but even if I haven't, I'm still excited to see my design as an actual, complete dress. The fabric won't come for about a week, but that works out perfectly—I'm scheduled to help my sister unpack and settle in, and my work for Vince is still slow enough to let me take some time off.

My phone alerts to let me know my car has arrived, so I turn out the lights and lock the door behind me. As I climb into the cab, I notice a short strand of thread clinging to my slacks, just above my knee. I pull it off, remembering the thread Logan pulled from my hair. The thought makes me smile.

———

I manage to avoid Logan all the next day. It helps that I slept until noon and that I didn't go up on the roof, but I'm still counting it a win. Around three in the afternoon I get a text from my sister.

RACHEL
Remind me never to move again

I've been binging *Outer Banks* on Netflix, but pause the show to reply.

TAYLOR
You're not allowed. I've already decided.

So are you here then?

RACHEL
Yup

TAYLOR
Yay!!

RACHEL
Are you still planning to come help me unpack?

TAYLOR
Of course! I don't need to be anywhere or do anything for at least a week, so I can even come and stay for a few days

RACHEL
That would be fantastic. Can you be here on Friday?

TAYLOR

Absolutely

RACHEL

Great. And you'll bring Logan, right? For the day at least?

I pause. Logan knows my sister is moving here, but I never got around to asking him to come and help. Besides, I still haven't worked through what happened at the studio yesterday, or how I feel about it.

TAYLOR

I actually haven't asked him yet. But since I'm going to stay for a few days I'll probably just come by myself.

I barely set my phone down and get up to find myself something to eat when she calls. I sigh, though I'm not surprised.

"Hey Rach," I say in a tired voice.

"What do you mean you haven't asked him yet? I told you our moving date weeks ago!"

"And I put it on my calendar, just like I said." I open the fridge, looking at what I have available.

"But you didn't talk to Logan."

"Nope."

"Why not?"

"Because I've had a lot of stuff going on and it hasn't come up, okay?"

There's a beat of silence, and then I hear her sigh.

"I know you better than anyone, T. And I can tell you have feelings for this guy."

I don't respond, just grab the milk and set it on the counter.

"Is it because he's a recovered alcoholic? Is that why you're trying to sabotage yourself?"

"It's because I have my career to think about," I say. The lie feels slimy on my tongue.

She sighs, giving up. "Fine. But T, I could really use his help."

I pause while reaching for the cereal above the fridge. "Why?"

"I wasn't here when the movers unloaded the truck, and they just dumped things wherever they could find room," she says. "Including the furniture. I don't know what Marc was thinking." She says the last part under her breath. "Anyway," she continues, her volume normal again, "it's more than even you and I can manage in a few days together. Marc is tied up at the hospital, and I'd really appreciate a stronger set of muscles, and another body, to help us move things around."

I've poured myself a bowl of Cheerios while she's been talking, chewing on her words as much as I am on the little O's. I swallow the bite in my mouth.

"Alright. I'll ask Logan if he's available to come with me," I say. Wanting Logan to come along because she desperately needs the extra help is a completely different reason than... well, whatever other reason I'd have for wanting him to come along.

"Really?" she says.

"Really. I'll ask him as soon as I get off the phone with you."

"Do you think he'll come? I mean, it's really short notice..."

"He'll come," I say, confident that the short notice won't deter him.

"Thanks, Taylor." I can hear the relief in her voice, as well as the sound of my nephew wailing in the background.

"You better go," I say. "I'll let you know when we're on our way Friday morning."

I end the call and finish my cereal, taking my time so I can avoid calling Logan for as long as possible. After washing my bowl and spoon by hand, drying them, and then putting them back in the cupboard, I finally pick up my phone and dial my neighbor's number. It rings once, twice...

"Hello?"

"Hey Logan, it's Taylor. I have a favor to ask."

Chapter 20

L ogan agrees to go with me, as I knew he would. He even offers to procure a car for us. I feel awkward on the other end of the phone, but he sounds as nonplussed as ever, and I begin to hope that the thing that happened at the studio wasn't a thing at all, and we can go back to being neighbor-friends-who-probably-like-each-other-but-won't-ever-get-together-because-I-have-issues.

I spend the next couple days working on the muslin for my dress. I get it sewn together and fit to my dress form, but I'm hesitant to try it on myself. I decide to take it with me and have my sister help me with the fit.

I get a text from Logan shortly after 8am on Friday, letting me know he's waiting outside in the car. I grab my overnight bag and my purse and head down the stairs. When I emerge from the building, a sleek, black Tesla is parked out front. Logan waves at me from the driver's seat.

"Nice ride," I say as he opens the door for me (because of course he got out to take my bag and be all chivalrous. Gah.).

"Thanks. Lynette said we could borrow it for the day."

"This is Lynette's car?"

"Yeah."

"And she doesn't need it?"

"Nah. Besides, she's got others at her disposal if she does."

I'm assuming Logan is referring to her fiancé, Dr. Hottie-what's-his-name. Thinking of them makes me think of the wedding, and my gut twists uncomfortably. It's not that I regret telling Logan I'll go with him, but ever since the studio, something undefined is making me nervous. Spending the day with Logan probably isn't going to help, but since he talks and acts as if nothing happened between us (because nothing *did* happen), I finally start to relax. It's probably just in my head.

In a little under two hours, we find ourselves pulling into the driveway of a large brick house in Randolph Township, New Jersey. As we follow the drive around to the garage, I see the front door burst open and a streak of purple racing down the walkway.

"An' Tayluh, An' Tayluh!"

Logan parks the car, and I laugh as my niece plows into the side of it, pressing her face and her palms against the passenger window. I see my sister coming around the corner from the front door, my one-year-old nephew on her hip. She looks more tired than usual, but I guess that's to be expected when you move across the country with two little ones in tow.

"An' Tayluh! Come an' see my bedwoom!" Grace calls, grabbing my hand with her chubby three-year-old paws as soon as I open the door.

"I'm coming, Gracie," I laugh. "Just give me a minute."

She dances around impatiently as I reach to give my sister a hug. "Oh Taylor, it's so good to see you!" she says. Liam squirms between us, grunting as he tries to push me away.

"You too. I can't believe you're finally here!" I give her one last squeeze and let her go.

"Thank you for coming out," Rachel says. "I'm sorry the guest room isn't really put together yet—we'll need to unpack some more boxes and try to find the sheets for the bed."

I wave her off. "That's the whole point of me coming. You can't possibly get a house unpacked and put together by yourself with these two underfoot." I hold my hands out for my nephew, but he burrows into my sister's neck.

Logan comes around the car to stand beside me. "You must be Logan," Rachel says, shifting her son and reaching out to shake his hand. "I've heard so much about you."

"Not *that* much," I say, narrowing my eyes at her in warning. She ignores me.

"I've heard a lot about you, too. Rachel, right?" Logan says.

"That's right. And this little guy is Liam," she says, bouncing her son on her hip. "Say 'hi' Liam." Liam stares at Logan for a minute and then shyly tucks his head into my sister's shoulder. Rachel smiles in apology, then moves toward the open garage. "Let's go through here, it's quicker. Don't mind the mess."

We maneuver through storage tubs and piles of shoes to the kitchen, where more than a dozen open boxes litter the floor and the countertops. Coming out the other side, we see a veritable mountain of boxes piled in the family room. The room is large and spacious—or it would be, if it wasn't completely filled with cardboard. A narrow path has been made through the chaos to allow access to the only piece of furniture in the room, a large gray sofa.

"As you can see, we're drowning in here," Rachel says, lifting an arm in defeat. "They dumped nearly all the boxes in here, and nearly all the furniture in there." She indicates the next room over, and a quick glance confirms her words. She sighs. "At least they put all the boxes marked 'kitchen' in the kitchen, but basically everything else is in here."

"So do you want us to start with the boxes or the furniture?" I ask.

"The boxes," she says, trying to shush Liam, who's fussing and pulling at her collar. "Just stack them in a corner of whatever room they go in so we can still get the furniture in there."

"Right," Logan says, his hands on his hips. "Are all the boxes labeled?"

"They should be," Rachel says. "But if they're not, just leave them in here and I'll sort them out." She turns to me with tired eyes. "I've got to feed Liam. Can you get started and I'll join you when I'm done?"

"Of course."

She settles into a corner of the couch, maneuvering Liam into position so she can nurse him. Logan is already sorting through a pile of boxes near the dining room, so I pick one up and check the label.

"'Books,'" I read, then look back at my sister. "Do you have a library? Or are they all going into Marc's office?"

"Both," she says. "But the rooms are connected. Just put them all in the library for now."

"And that is...?"

"The office is upstairs, first door on the left. The library is through the closet in the office."

Logan looks up from stacking boxes. "A secret room?"

Rachel smiles. "Yeah. Marc was excited about that, too."

Logan looks at me, anticipation plastered all over his grin. "Let's check it out."

I shift the box of books in my arms. "Lead the way."

Logan picks up another box marked 'books' and we head up the stairs. Unfortunately, our way is blocked at the top by a scowling toddler with her hands on her hips.

"An' Tayluh! Why didun you come? I'm waiting!"

"Looks like someone's in trouble," Logan says over his shoulder.

"Grace, sweetie, I'm sorry, I had to talk to your mom first. Can we get by, please?"

Glaring as only a three-year-old tyrant can, Grace steps aside to let us come upstairs, but she grabs my arm before I can move past her.

"Come see my woom," she says.

"I will, honey, I promise. Just let me put this box down."

She gives me a dirty look, not letting go of my arm. "No, come *now*."

"Hey Grace," Logan says, "do you think you could help us? See, we're trying to find a secret room..."

That does the trick. Grace immediately drops my arm, jumping excitedly.

"I know where it is!" she says. "Follow me!"

Logan grins as we turn to follow her. "Good thinking," I murmur.

We walk through an open door to the left, then follow Grace into the spacious walk-in closet of the office. "Thwoo here," she says, pushing on a section of wall that opens into another room.

Floor to ceiling bookshelves in a dark, rich wood line two of

160

the four walls. Three large windows on the other walls let in plenty of natural light, and the cream carpet underfoot is thick and luxurious. Logan lets out a low whistle.

"Ta-da!" Grace says, twirling in the middle of the room.

"This is amazing," Logan says. "I wonder how many books would fit in here?"

"Thank you, Grace," I say, setting my box down near the shelves. "Now, why don't you show me your room?"

My niece needs no further invitation. Grabbing my hand, she pulls me back through the door. "I'll see you back downstairs," I call to Logan.

———

After getting a thorough tour from Grace of not only her bedroom but the entire house, I manage to extricate myself and head back into the overstuffed family room. I'm amazed at how many boxes Logan has already managed to move while I've been entertaining my niece.

"Oh good, you're back," my sister says. She's still on the couch, cradling her now-sleeping son in her arms.

"Sorry, Grace got ahold of me."

"That's fine. It's just that Logan said there are a bunch of boxes marked 'bedroom,' but it doesn't identify *which* bedroom. Can you open them up and tell me what's inside, so I can tell you which bedroom they go in?

"Sure," I say. "Do you have a knife?"

"Here," Logan says from behind me, and I turn around. He's come back for more boxes and is holding out a small, folded knife to me.

"Oh. Thanks," I say, taking it from him.

"Logan's been sorting what he can find," Rachel says. "All those boxes over there," she points, "say 'bedroom.' Everything else he's putting into piles and taking them to where they belong."

"So how many bedrooms are boxed up? And which ones are they?"

Logan looks up, paying attention.

"The guest room is down here, on the other side of the kitchen," she says. "The master is at the top of the stairs on the right. You already know where the office is, and that leaves Grace's room and the nursery."

"Which are upstairs at the end of the hall, right?" I ask.

"Right. So if you open up a box and let me know what's inside it—"

"You can tell me which room it's for and I'll write it on the box," I finish. "Do you have a Sharpie?"

She shakes her head.

"That's fine," I say. "I'll just sort them into piles."

"And then I can take them all to where they belong," Logan adds.

"Thank you so much," Rachel says. "That would be great."

We spend the next hour working as a three-man team. As I open each box and describe the contents to my sister, she tells me which room it's for and I move it to the appointed pile. Logan keeps going back and forth, up and down, hauling boxes to their respective rooms in the house. Every so often I hear him chuckle or mutter to himself, and I notice that he has one earbud in.

"What are you listening to?" I finally ask.

"An audiobook," he says, picking up another box and leaving the room again.

"He's a reader?" Rachel asks.

I shrug. "I guess so. He was reading *Pride and Prejudice* on the train to the flower show," I say, slicing open another box.

"*Pride and Prejudice*? Seriously?"

"Seriously." I glance inside the box. "Looks like sheets, candles, a few books—"

"Guest room," she says. "That's lucky, you'll need the sheets to make your bed tonight."

I push the box towards the dining room, then crouch down beside another one and open it.

"So how is work?" she asks.

"Fine. I've just been working on some staples while I wait for Vince to give me another custom assignment," I reply, noting the toys in the box and shoving it towards the others bound for Grace's room. "I've got some ideas floating around for Fashion Week, but I'll have to talk to him before I really flesh any of them out."

She shakes her head, grinning. "Fashion Week. I can't believe it."

I let out a breathless laugh. "Me neither. I still have to pinch myself sometimes."

"What's it like to work with him?"

"Vince? It's... fine." When she doesn't reply, I glance over at her, then laugh at the look she gives me. "Ok, it's not all sunshine and roses. He's a bit of a diva, and some of his ideas are a little out there, but overall..." I let the sentence trail off, and the little worrisome voice raises it's head in the back of my mind and sniffs the air.

"But?" my sister prompts.

"But overall it's fine. Really."

She gives me another look, and I sigh. "I just can't help

feeling like there's something I'm missing," I say. "Something I should know. I feel uneasy about some things, like what happened to his previous designer? And why won't he credit me for my work?"

"Have you asked?"

"I've tried, but haven't had much success." I shrug. "I don't know. Maybe I'm just *foreboding joy*. It still seems too good to be true, you know?"

She nods, and wiggles her way to the edge of the couch before standing, glancing inside the box I've just opened. "That's for the master bedroom. I'm going to go lay Liam down for a nap and then fix us some lunch," she says while I move the box to its respective pile. "Why don't you and Logan start unpacking the books in the library? Tell him he can organize them however he wants."

She heads off to put her son down while I place the box with the others marked for the master bedroom. I look around for any more boxes marked 'books,' but it looks like Logan may have found and moved them all already. Either that, or they're buried under the boxes still piled across the room.

Not wanting to go upstairs empty-handed, I grab a box marked 'office' and head for the stairs, just as Logan comes back into the room.

"Rachel is putting Liam down for a nap," I say. "She wants us to unpack the books in the library."

He frowns. "Where does she want us to put them?"

"I would assume on the bookshelves," I say, smirking at him.

He rolls his eyes. "Ha, ha. I meant, how does she want them organized?"

I shrug. "She said you can sort them however you like."

He stares at me for half a second, then slowly shakes his head. "You two are obviously not book people," he says, before grabbing the box I just placed in the master bedroom pile. "But I guess we'll take a stab at it."

Chapter 21

W hen we reach the top of the stairs, we find Grace
arguing with her mom.

"But I don' *wanna* take a nap!" she whines. "I'm not tired. I
wanna help An' Tayluh."

"Aunt Taylor is going to unpack some boxes with her
friend. *You* are going to have some lunch and then take a nap,
missy. You can play with her after that."

Grace starts to protest again, but Rachel picks her up and
marches down the stairs. Logan deposits his box in the master
bedroom while I take mine into the office, then we both duck
through the closet door into the library.

I have to admit, there's something a bit magical about the
hidden room. Even without being a 'book person,' I can see the
appeal of having somewhere quiet and secluded to go when I
want to be alone.

Logan is kneeling next to a box, and he reaches a hand out
toward me. Without thinking, I put my hand in his. Surprise
flits across his face, and then he chuckles.

"I was holding my hand out for the knife, Taylor," he says.

"Oh!" I snatch my hand back, heat rushing into my cheeks. "Um, I left it downstairs. I'll go get it."

I rush from the room, feeling mortified. What on earth was I thinking? Why did I give him my hand? My insides churn with embarrassment as I head back to the family room where I left the knife.

I find it on the floor next to the dwindling pile of boxes marked 'bedroom.' I pick it up, turning it over in my hand. But my cheeks are still burning, so instead of going back upstairs, I head to the kitchen.

I find my sister making grilled cheese sandwiches. She looks up when I come in the room, then points the spatula in her hand at the small stack of sandwiches on the plate beside her.

"Nothing fancy, I'm afraid," she says. "But help yourself. Where's Logan?"

"Still upstairs. I had to come down for the knife."

She frowns. "Did you find it?"

I pull out a barstool and sit down at the counter, looking at her. "Yeah. I did."

"Then why—" She stops, searching my face. Abruptly she turns off the stove, removes the pan, and turns to her daughter. "Are you about finished, sweetie? It's time for you to take a nap."

Grace is seated at the nearby table, eating the last remnants of her lunch. "I don' wanna take a nap," she says around a mouthful of bread. "I wanna pway wiff An' Tayluh."

"Aunt Taylor will be with us for a few days—you'll have plenty of time to play with her later. Come on."

Rachel rinses a rag at the sink and wipes Grace's hands and

face. Picking up the still protesting toddler, she gives me a pointed look. "Don't go anywhere, I'll be right back."

I nod, and they leave the room. A few minutes later my sister returns.

"What happened? Are you ok?"

"No," I groan, pressing a hand to my forehead. "I gave him my hand."

"What?" she asks, confused.

I sigh. "We were up in the library with all the boxes of books. Logan held out his hand for the knife, but I didn't *know* that's what he was doing, so I put my hand in his."

Her eyebrows shoot up, and her mouth pulls into a grin. "Oh! Well. Why did you do that?"

"I have no idea," I say, folding my arms on the counter and laying my head against them. "It just... happened."

All the embarrassment comes rushing back to me as I explain, and I'm afraid to lift my head and look at her, afraid to see her teasing smile and knowing eyes. But she doesn't say anything. Instead, I hear the stool next to mine slide across the floor and feel her put her arms around me.

"How are you feeling?" she asks gently.

"Embarrassed. Awkward. Confused." I lift my head and look at her, into the soft brown eyes I know so well. "What was I thinking? Why did I do that?"

She shifts beside me. "I don't know. What *were* you thinking?"

"Nothing. I wasn't thinking, I just acted."

"Hmm." She's quiet for a minute. "Do you normally put your hand in other people's if they hold it out to you?"

"Not unless it's a handshake."

She nods. "Right, but if it wasn't? Like if one of your old

168

coworkers held his hand out to you, palm up, what would you do?"

"I'd look at him like he was crazy and ask what he wanted."

She hides a smile. "And what if I held my hand out to you?"

And then she does. She holds out her hand to me, palm up, an expectant smile on her face. I look at her, and then at her hand, and then back at her. My heart starts to race, and slowly I reach my own hand out and put it in hers. Ours palms wrap around each other, and she gives my hand a gentle squeeze.

"I'd give you my hand," I say quietly.

"You would. I know you would. And do you know why?"

I've been staring at our hands hanging between us, but at her question I look up, fear suddenly gripping my chest.

"Because you love me. And trust me," she says gently.

My pulse is pounding in my ears now, and I barely hear her quiet words. "Are you saying—" I start to ask, but she cuts me off.

"I'm not saying anything," she says. "Except that I know why you put your hand in mine when I hold it out to you."

She gives my hand another squeeze and gets up from the stool. "Logan is probably wondering where you are with the knife," she says, going back around the counter. "I'll save you some sandwiches."

———

When I get back to the library, I find Logan sitting cross-legged on the floor in the middle of the room, leaning over a large book in his lap. A box is open beside him, and a few other books are stacked nearby as well.

Whether he sees or hears me first I'm not sure, but he glances up at me as I duck through the door.

"Hi," he says. "Did you find the knife?"

"Yeah, I just... got to talking with Rachel." I frown. "How did you get the box open without the knife?"

"Oh, I just peeled off the tape," he says. "I had to pick at the edge for a bit, but once the corner lifted it was easy."

"Ah. So what are you reading?"

He flips the book closed so he can read the cover. "*Priory of the Orange Tree.* It looked and sounded interesting, so I figured I might as well read a bit while I waited for you. And then it sucked me in."

He puts it down and smiles up at me. "Should we try this again?" He holds out his hand, and I place the closed knife in his palm.

"Are you sure you don't want to hold my hand?" he teases.

I answer him by smacking his shoulder. He laughs, reaching for another box to open.

"So how do you want to organize them?" I ask, hoping to change the subject.

He surveys the sea of cardboard around us, then glances up at the shelves. "Not sure. First I'd like to see what they have."

Logan starts cutting open the boxes, and together we pull out the contents. Most of them contain books similar in size to each other, but sometimes there are random other books thrown in to fill the space. As we unpack, Logan begins to sort them into piles, and soon I'm calling out authors and titles, or sometimes whole genres for him. Most of the boxes contain medical books, but there are a fair number of novels, biographies, and children's books as well. Every so often Logan will ask for a stack near me and move them to another pile.

"Wow, these are old," I say, pulling out some books with threadbare covers and worn, dark pages. "Looks like we have Tennyson, Eighteenth Century English Poetry and Prose, and something about Confucius?" Logan holds his hands out for them and I pass them over.

I open another box. "I didn't realize you liked to read so much," I say, noticing the contents are all medical texts and shoving the box to the farthest, largest pile. "What kind of books? I mean, besides *Pride and Prejudice*," I tease.

He shrugs. "I'm not picky. I love a good story, and I'm fascinated by people and history. So I read both novels and nonfiction."

"What about self-help?"

He feigns a look of offense. "Taylor, I'm insulted. Are you saying I have faults?"

"Ha," I pull out a few small paperbacks from another box, placing them in the appropriate pile.

"I've read a few self improvement books, but not many. *Atomic Habits* was pretty great, but I couldn't get through *Everything About You Is Wrong*. It was way too depressing. And once I tried to read *How To Win Friends and Influence People*, but gave up pretty quick."

"It's not like you'd need that book anyway," I say. "You seem to make friends with everyone, everywhere."

I don't know why I said that. I mean, it's true, but it's certainly not helping eliminate the flames of embarrassment licking up my neck again. I clear my throat, trying not to notice how intently he's watching me.

"So Taylor," Logan says, opening another box, "can I ask you a question?"

171

My heart skitters a moment before thumping painfully in my chest. "I have a feeling you're going to ask, even if I say no."

"That's not true," he says, and I hear a note of—concern? hurt?—in his voice. But I just shrug.

"Go ahead," I say, trying to sound nonchalant.

But he doesn't say anything. After a few minutes, I start to relax, hoping he changed his mind.

I pick up a couple paperbacks. "Where do you want books about—"

"Why did you give me your hand earlier?" he blurts out, cutting me off.

Heat rushes to my face again, and I force out a laugh to hide my embarrassment. "Oh, that. It was a knee-jerk reaction. I thought you were reaching out because you needed help standing up or something."

But I can tell he doesn't believe me. Heck, I don't even believe myself. But what am I supposed to say to him? Ignoring the guilt bubbling in my gut, I shove a box toward him. "Last one," I say, trying desperately to think of a way to change the subject before he can ask me again.

Logan opens the box and starts pulling out the books inside. I watch him, wondering what he's thinking, until he glances up at me... and then I know *exactly* what he's thinking.

"So what were you listening to earlier?" I ask, starting to panic. "You said it was an audiobook, but you didn't name it."

"It's a book by J.K. Rowling," he says mildly, reading the spines on the books remaining in the box.

"One of the Harry Potter books?"

"No, actually. It's called *The Christmas Pig.*"

I look over at him, not sure I heard him right. "*The Christmas Pig?*"

"Yup." He reaches for another pile.

"Huh. Never heard of it."

"It's a great book. One of my favorites, actually." He's starting to thaw, and inwardly I relax.

"But why are you reading it now? It's July."

"Haven't you ever heard of Christmas in July?"

"Oh no," I moan, "Don't tell me you're one of those Christmas fanatics, too."

He smiles. "What do you have against Christmas?"

"Nothing. But it belongs in December, when it's cold and snowy; not in the middle of summer."

"You know, in Australia, Christmas *does* fall in the middle of the summer."

"Do you see any kangaroos around here?"

He laughs, and the sound sends my insides swooping. "Fair enough," he says, his eyes crinkling at the corners. "But that's the only time I'll let you win that argument."

His words send a funny ripple through my body. What a strange way to say that. Does he mean we'll be having the same argument another time? Again and again? Like an old, married couple? Before I can panic too much over what he meant, he speaks again.

"I wouldn't say I'm a Christmas *fanatic*, exactly, but I don't discriminate against holiday enthusiasts. And I'm not opposed to reading Christmas books year round "

"Apparently."

Logan gets to his feet and surveys the shelves, his hands on his hips. "Where to start," he murmurs.

"How about with the biggest pile?" I point to the clustered stacks of medical volumes to our right. It makes up at least a third of all the books we've unpacked.

"Actually, that's not a bad idea. Why don't you start on those while I figure out where to put the rest."

"Sounds good. I'll put them on the far shelves, closest to Marc's office."

"Perfect," he says.

I start looking through the medical books, trying to decide how best to organize them. It's silent for a few minutes as we each get our bearings, but just as I begin to put the largest books on the bottommost shelf, I hear Logan's voice behind me.

"We can listen to it together, if you want," he says.

I turn around, confused. "Listen to what?"

"The book I was listening to earlier. *The Christmas Pig.*"

I grab another tome from the pile and place it next to the others on the shelf. "It sounds like a kids' book," I hedge.

"You know, some of the finest literature ever written was created for children," he says.

I roll my eyes, but can't help the grin that tugs on my mouth. Why does he have that effect on me? I immediately frown.

"Come on," he says, reaching in his pocket for the other earbud. "I think you'll enjoy it. I'll even start it over, so you won't miss anything."

He holds out the earbud and I take it from him, placing it in my ear. He scrolls on his phone for a minute, then I hear the narrator begin to speak.

"Can you hear it ok?" Logan asks.

I nod, and we both turn back to the bookshelves. "I think I'll separate them by genre, and then arrange them alphabetically by last name," he muses, while the narrator hums the opening credits in our ears.

We settle into silence—me working on the seemingly

endless pile of medical texts, Logan sorting through the half-dozen other piles. I watch him out of the corner of my eye as he picks up a stack and places it carefully on the shelf. Then he moves them around until he's satisfied with their order. Every so often he starts leafing through the pages of a book, stopping to read a page or two, and every smile and quiet chuckle makes me curious. Eventually he catches me watching him and I quickly look away, focusing on my own pile of books. I don't look at him again, and soon the story of DP and Jack captures my attention completely.

Chapter 22

It takes Logan and I about an hour to get all the books on the shelves. Rachel interrupts us halfway through chapter four to remind us to come eat some lunch. I ask Logan if we can keep listening while we eat, as much to avoid talking to him as because I'm enjoying the story. He seems happy at the request, and even though I feel myself getting quieter and more withdrawn throughout the day, he seems as cheerful as ever. Perhaps more so, if I'm being honest.

But I don't want to be honest right now. At least not with myself.

The conversation with my sister in the kitchen has left me thinking and feeling all kinds of things, and I can't sort them out here. Until I get home to New York and can be by myself, I just need to survive. And not let anything else weird happen between my neighbor and I.

Logan and I move boxes and furniture until seven in the evening. We get through about two-thirds of the story by dinnertime (pizza delivery), but then we decide to stop it so we can pay better attention to what we're doing. Finally, when

Rachel asks for my help bathing the kids and tucking them into bed, Logan says he's going to head back to the city.

"Thank you so much for all your help," Rachel says, stepping forward with her arms open. Logan doesn't hesitate to hug her, which surprises me for some reason. I'm not much of a hugger myself, but somehow it makes me glad to know that Logan is.

"Anytime," he says. "It was fun." Then, turning to me, "You'll be back on Sunday, right?"

"Monday, actually," I say. "I told Rachel I'd stay for three nights." I look to my sister, and she gives me a grateful smile. "But then I've got to get back and do some work."

"I guess I'll see you Monday, then," he says, smiling. For one moment I can almost see in his eyes the desire to step forward and hug me, too, but of course he doesn't. I don't know if I'm more relieved or disappointed, and the uncertainty gnaws at me.

After Logan leaves, I help Rachel bathe her kids and get them in their pjs. I read a story to Grace while my sister nurses Liam and puts him down, and after several failed attempts, I manage to convince Grace to stay in her room and *not* keep creeping down the stairs to find me.

I'm making up the bed in the guest room when my sister comes down. "Thanks for getting Grace to bed," she says, stopping in the doorway.

"No problem."

"How did you manage it?"

"Oh, the usual—threats, followed by bribery. Let's hope it works."

She laughs quietly. "What did you offer her?"

"I told her that if she stays in bed, I'll draw up a pretty dress in the morning, designed especially for her," I say, spreading a quilt out on top of the sheets.

"Oo, a Taylor O'Neill original," Rachel says, leaning against the doorway. "That's definitely worth staying in bed."

"Let's hope," I say with a chuckle, plumping a pillow before tossing it on the bed. "Because one of these nights, I need your help to fit the muslin for my orchid dress."

"Orchid dress?"

"That's what I'm calling the dress I'm making for myself. The design was inspired by one of the orchids I saw at the flower show in the spring, so I'm calling it my orchid dress." I shrug. "I got it fitted to my sewing mannequin, but I'd like to try it on myself and see if it needs adjusting."

"Sure, I'd love to help you with that."

"Great."

With the bed made, I start unpacking a few things from my bag. Rachel comes in and sits down on the edge of the bed, beside the pillows. "So?" she asks without preamble.

I don't have to ask what she's referring to, but I also don't want to have this conversation. I'm not ready. "So what?" I say, putting my toiletry bag on a stack of boxes near the window.

"So did you talk with Logan at all?"

"Sure, we talked about a lot of stuff."

She picks up a pillow and throws it at me. It hits me on the shoulder and knocks me off balance, but I catch myself.

"We didn't talk about what happened. Or how I feel," I say. "Happy?"

She frowns. "Of course not," she says.

"Well, sorry to disappoint, but there it is."

I pull out a few more things from my bag—a pair of pjs, my phone charger, curl cream—and set them on the bed. Rachel doesn't say anything, but I know my sister—it's just a matter of time before she brings it up again.

"Have you at least *thought* about it?" she asks at last.

I throw my hands up in exasperation. "Of course I've thought about it! How could I *not* think about it after what you said to me earlier?" I sigh, sitting down on the opposite side of the bed. "But what am I supposed to do? I can't... I mean, I don't... uuugh."

I fall forward onto the bed, burying my face in the quilt. Rachel reaches over and strokes my hair, letting the silence swell between us . "Have you ever been in love, Taylor?" she asks after a while.

I groan incoherently.

"It's not something you plan for. It's not something you expect. Sometimes it just happens, and when it does, you have to let it."

"No, I don't," I say, abruptly sitting up. "I have worked too hard for too long to let anything get in my way."

"Are you sure that's the only reason?"

"Yes."

My jaw is set, and I can feel the ferocity in my gaze as I say the lie, but my sister is looking at me in a way I don't ever remember her looking at me before. Her face is more sad than angry, but there's a hint of both emotions in her eyes—it's not quite disapproval, it's more like...

Disappointment.

"Look," I say, feeling defensive. "Logan is a great guy. He really is. But he's only been sober for four years—what if he cracks? What if he becomes an alcoholic again?"

"Taylor, you can't—"

"I can and I will, Rachel. I'm not going through that again."

I take a deep breath, pushing down the panic that is starting to build in my chest, clinging to the safety of my career-driven persona. "Besides, I'm so close I can taste it," I say, dropping onto the bed with a sigh. "Whatever this is with Logan is just going to have to wait. I can't lose this job with Vince, Rach, I just can't. It's my only chance."

"And if that's not the real reason you're pushing him away?"

The icy knot behind my breastbone won't loosen, and I don't trust myself to speak. She stares at me for a long time, then slowly gets up. She goes across the room and retrieves the pillow she threw at me, places it back on the bed, then crosses to the door. Turning back, she says, "Sometimes love doesn't wait, Taylor. Sometimes you only get one chance." She sighs. "Come on. Let's get started on the living room."

Chapter 23

G race didn't get out of bed again, so in the morning I draw up a sketch for her as promised.

"Make it pink, An' Tayluh," she demands, leaning over the table.

"I don't have my pencils with me, Gracie," I say. "But you can color it in with your crayons."

She scowls. "Momma packed dem in a box."

"Well, then you'll just have to imagine that it's pink," I say, adding a ruffle to the hemline of the full skirt.

I sign my name with a flourish and tear out the sheet of paper, handing it to her. She squeals in delight."

"Thank you, An' Tayluh!" She hugs my leg and runs off.

Rachel and I spend the day unpacking boxes and organizing the house. I play with my niece (and nephew, when he lets me) and chat with Marc over dinner. Sunday is more of the same, and in the evening Rachel helps me with my dress.

"Oh, Taylor," she says as I slip into the muslin. "What a beautiful silhouette."

"Thanks," I say, turning in a circle. "Now, can you pin up the back so we can mark the edge?"

I hold still while she pins the fabric in place. "This is going to look phenomenal, T," she says. "Are you going to save it for a special occasion?"

"Not exactly," I say, measuring my words. "When I initially decided to make the design, I didn't have a particular event or occasion in mind. But I actually have a wedding at the end of the month, so I'm going to wear it to that."

"It may be a bit fancy for a wedding, don't you think?"

"The invitation said black tie."

"Oh, well, I guess—" She gasps. "Is it that celebrity wedding you told me about? The one that Vince is going to?"

I laugh. "Josh Pratt? No, I'm not invited to that one."

"So whose wedding?"

I sigh in defeat. "It's one of Logan's friends. I'm going as his plus one."

Rachel grabs the top of my arms and turns me around to face her. "What? When did this happen?"

"It's not a big deal. We stablished that we're just going as friends."

"Taylor, listen to yourself!" She throws her hands up. "That's a *date*, Taylor. You agreed to go to *a formal wedding* with the guy. How can you not see this?"

"I told you, we established—"

"Taylor." My sister's look has melted from exasperation to one of deep concern. "I can't tell you what to think or feel. But do you realize what you're doing to Logan?"

Her seriousness startles me. "What do you mean?"

"That man is head over heels for you, Taylor. You have to see that."

I roll my eyes and turn my back to her, indicating that she should continue pinning. "He is not. It's just a crush, and he knows perfectly well that I don't want a relationship. He's known all along."

"What he knows has practically no bearing on what he *feels*, Taylor—you of all people should understand that. Even a blind man could see that he feels a lot more than friendship for you. And after what happened in the library... well, the guy is going to hope. And hope is a hard thing to kill."

I don't reply, not wanting to continue this conversation.

I hear my sister sigh, but she doesn't say anything else as she continues to pin the fabric up the length of my back. "There," she says after another minute. "That's all."

I walk into the small adjoining bathroom to look in the mirror. Rachel follows but stops in the doorway, crossing her arms. I turn first one way and then the other, trying to see how the muslin fits from various angles.

"I think I need to take in the shoulders a bit more," I say.

"Is there a way I can mark that for you?"

"Yeah, can you grab my marking pen from off the bed?"

She retrieves the pen and hands it to me. I demonstrate on the back of her own shoulder what to feel for and where I need her to mark the fabric, and then I turn my back to her so she can mark the muslin for me.

"Both shoulders, please," I say, "in the same spot."

She finishes and I turn back around. "I think that might be all it needs," I murmur to myself."

Still, my sister isn't speaking, and I'm beginning to worry that something might be seriously wrong. I turn to face her.

"What is it, Rachel—what are you trying not to say?"

"I just worry," she says. "I worry that you're being stubborn

183

and inflexible, and that it's going to hurt Logan and cost you your friendship." She shrugs. "But there's nothing else I can say to make you see what I see. That's all."

We stare at each other for a long moment, until I turn to pick up the marking pen and hand it to my sister. "Would you please mark the seam lines—where the fabric overlaps—along the back, please? Then I can take this off and we can do some more unpacking."

She takes the pen without a word and I turn away from her, trying to forget the things she said and the look on her face when she said them.

———

The next morning I get a text from Logan, just as I'm finishing breakfast.

LOGAN

Hey, do you know what time you're coming home?

TAYLOR

This afternoon. Marc is going to drop me off before his shift tonight.

LOGAN

Awesome. Send me a text when you're on your way, k?

TAYLOR

Why?

LOGAN

🙂

I roll my eyes and set my phone down, taking another bite of toasted bagel. What is he up to this time?

Rachel and I have unpacked and organized most of the house by the time I have to leave at three. I gather my things and give Grace a piggy back ride to the garage. The rest of the family is already there.

"Thanks so much for coming over, T," Rachel says, giving me a hug as Marc puts my bag in the car.

"Of course," I say. "Anytime."

"An' Tayluh, why can't you stay?" Grace says, pulling on my arm. I crouch down to look her in the eyes.

"Because I have to go back home so I can work," I say. "But you live so close to me now, that I'll get to see you lots and lots."

"Really?"

"Yup. I'll come visit you and you can come visit me."

She grins and wraps her arms around me. When I finally stand up, Rachel gives me another hug. "Tell Logan thanks again."

"I will."

"He's a great guy, Taylor."

"I know."

"You should give him a chance."

"We tried that with Dad."

"This is *nothing* like—"

"'Bye, Rach," I say, getting inside the car before she can say anything else.

She makes a show of rolling her eyes, but as we pull out of the driveway she picks up Grace so they can both wave to me. I wave back until we turn onto the street and they're lost from view.

Marc is a quiet guy, and content to let me listen to music or read on my phone while we drive. He turns on talk radio, and after texting Logan I pull up my email.

There's one from Amelia, letting me know they finished some pieces for Vince and will have the final fitting tomorrow. And there's one from Vince, inviting me to lunch with him and his assistant to discuss his look for Fashion Week. A little thrill shoots through me as I read the words. *I'll be designing what Vince wears to Fashion Week!*

I ask Marc about his new job and we pass some time talking about life in New York.

"You have no idea how excited Rachel is to be living so close to you," he says as we make our way across The Narrows. "She's been talking about it for months."

"I still can't believe you guys are here," I say. "I'm looking forward to watching Grace and Liam grow up."

"Don't blink," he says wryly, "or you'll miss it."

We make it to my apartment building shortly after five.

"Thanks so much for all your help," he says as he pulls up along the curb.

"Anytime," I say. "Seriously, if you need anything, please let me know."

"I'll take you up on that. I'd love to take your sister away for our anniversary in a few months, if you feel up to taking the kids."

"Absolutely. Just let me know when so I can put it on my calendar."

He waves and drives off, back to Newark for the night shift. Hitching my bag further up my shoulder, I climb up the stairs to my apartment. As I approach the landing, I see a small square of yellow paper fluttering just above my doorknob, and I grin, anticipation lighting up my insides.

Meet me on the roof

I shouldn't be so excited to get Logan's note, not with all the drama and confusion whirling inside me, but I can't help it. Dropping my stuff inside, I head straight up the stairs.

It's hot on the roof, and so bright I have to squint and shade my eyes. There, under a pop up canopy, sits Logan. He's seated on a red blanket spread out over a square of astroturf, next to an inflatable lawn decoration of Santa. Strings of colored lights hang from the edges of the canopy, though the sun is so bright I can barely see them glowing.

I stop, shocked at the sight.

A small artificial Christmas tree is also set up under the canopy, with garlands of red and gold festooning the branches. Underneath the tree is a wrapped gift, and on the other side of Logan is a small cooler. I can hear the song *Mele Kalikimaka* coming from somewhere, and despite my surprise at it all, a slow grin spreads across my face as I walk towards the canopy.

"What's all this?" I ask.

Logan stood up as soon as he saw me, and now he spreads his arms wide, grinning at me. "Welcome to Christmas in July, Taylor."

I laugh, looking around. "I can see that, but why?"

He shrugs, still smiling. "Just for fun. I thought it would be a good joke, you know, considering what we talked about at your sister's."

His mention of our conversation in the library makes my stomach flip, but I ignore the sensation. "This is..." I search for the right word.

"Amazing? Fantastic? Fun?"

"Ridiculous," I say with a laugh, "but it's great. I just can't believe it."

"Believe it," he says. "Oh, and look!" He points to the wrapped gift under the Christmas tree. "It wouldn't be Christmas without presents."

"What is it?"

"You'll see. But for now, are you hungry? I have some deli sandwiches and cold lemonade in the cooler."

We sit down, and for the first time I notice a book lying on the corner of the blanket. "What's that?" I ask.

"Oh, it's *The Christmas Pig*—the one we were listening to at your sister's house?" He picks up the book and turns it over in his hands so I can see the cover. "I know we didn't get to finish it, so I wanted to offer to let you borrow it if you'd like. I marked the chapter where we left off."

He holds it out to me, but when I reach to take it from him he doesn't let go. I look up at his face, a question in my eyes.

"Before I lend you this book, there's something I have to tell you."

His look is intense, and my heart starts racing as his eyes search mine. They flick down to my mouth and back up again, so quickly I wonder if I imagined it. But the flush of red at his neck tells me I didn't, and my own warm cheeks aren't just because of the heat.

"Yes?" I ask, trying to ignore the fluttering in my stomach.

"If you fold the corner of a page down to mark your spot instead of using a bookmark, I'll never speak to you again."

I blink at him—at his serious eyes and somber expression, and then we both burst out laughing. It diffuses the tense bubble that filled the space between us, and relief washes through me. This is so much easier. *This* is what I want, I tell myself.

"Come on, let's eat," he says, opening the cooler and handing me a paper-wrapped sandwich.

So we drink cold lemonade and eat sandwiches and chips from the deli the next block over. He asks about Rachel's family and I tell him all the things we were able to get done on the house.

"Rachel says thanks again," I tell him, finishing the last bite of my sandwich.

"Tell her she is very welcome," he replies. Wiping his hands on a napkin, he reaches for the present under the tree. He smiles, big enough to reveal the cleft in his chin and the one dimple in his cheek, and hands it to me.

"This is for you," he says.

It's small, about the size of a child's shoebox, and doesn't weigh very much. The wrapping paper is blue with white snowflakes, and one of those premade bows of white curling ribbon is attached to the top. Logan is clearly excited for me to open it, and my curiosity is definitely piqued.

I shake it gently and feel something shift inside. "What is it?"

He groans. "Please tell me you're not a gift-shaker."

"What, you're not?"

"Oh, I'm totally a shaker, I just want you to open it already!"

I laugh and tear off the paper, revealing a box of Barillo pasta. "Ignore the box," he says. "It's all I could find in my apartment."

Slipping my finger underneath the bit of tape keeping the

flap closed, I open the box. Tipping it over, I let what's inside fall out.

A silken pile of lacy cloth drops into my hand, the color of fresh-churned butter. The open weave is incredibly detailed, and as I gently pick it up, I can see designs of flowers and leaves intricately woven throughout.

"Oh wow," I breathe, holding the lace between my outstretched arms.

"Do you like it?" he asks.

"It's stunning," I say. Suddenly I gasp. "Logan, did you make this?"

"I did." He's smiling bigger than I've seen him smile in months, the excitement and pride he feels nearly palpable.

Awed, I move it gently through my fingers. "It's absolutely beautiful," I say. "I can't believe you made this."

"It's a fashion scarf," he says, taking the lace carefully out of my hands. "I started it shortly after the flower show, as a sort of memento, you know?"

We're still sitting on the ground, and as he scoots closer to me, our knees touch. My heart starts pounding at his nearness. Holding the scarf between his hands, he rises up on his knees, draping it around the back of my neck. My face brushes against his shirt, and I inhale, the scent of heat and soap and men's shaving cream filling my nostrils. He sits back on his heels, taking one end of the short scarf and letting it drop down across my chest, draping the other end just over my shoulder.

"Perfect," he says, his breath caressing my cheek.

I hardly hear what he says, my heart is pounding so loudly in my ears.

"Do you like it?" he asks.

I can't seem to tear my eyes away from his. "Y-yes," I murmur. "It's beautiful."

His face is inches from mine, and as he glances down at my mouth he brings his hand up to cup my cheek.

"Taylor," he breathes.

I know that if I lean forward, towards him, he'll kiss me. But I'm too afraid of what might happen if I let him do that, so I lean back instead.

The abrupt movement startles Logan and he nearly loses his balance. "Oh!" I squeak. "Sorry, I just, um..." My face feels hot, and I scramble to pull my jumbled thoughts together. I pull away again, more slowly this time. "Thanks, Logan. I love it. The scarf. It's great."

The words come out disjointed and robotic. Logan sits back, his face as flushed as mine feels. "Yeah, of course. I'm glad you like it." He clears his throat, then gets to his feet.

I stand as well, feeling awkwardly miserable, not knowing what to do. Logan starts cleaning up, looking everywhere but at me.

"Do you want some help taking the decorations down?" I ask.

"No, no, it's fine, I've got it. It won't take long." He's facing away from me, the back of his neck still scarlet.

"Okay." I watch him for another minute, feeling worse by the second. "Um... can I take the book?" I ask, more for something to say, anything to say, than because I actually want to read it.

"Of course. I said you could borrow it."

He still won't look at me, rushing around unplugging lights and throwing out bits of paper, so I crouch down and pick up the book. It feels heavy and hot in my hand, even though it's not very big.

"Okay. I guess... I guess I'll see you later then."

"See ya," he calls, his back to me.

"Thanks for the picnic. And the scarf," I call, in a final, desperate effort to get him to look at me.

But he doesn't. He waves a hand in the air, still not turning around. "Sure thing."

I turn and walk slowly back to my apartment. Once inside, I head down the short hall to my bedroom, to look in the mirror. The scarf is still draped around my neck the way Logan arranged it, and as I reach my hand up to finger the silken stitches, I sigh.

"What was I thinking," I murmur. "What was *he* thinking?"

Carefully I remove the scarf and place it gently on my dresser. Leaving my room, I go to collect my overnight bag, wondering if I've managed to ruin everything.

Chapter 24

Logan texts me later that evening, just as I'm getting in bed.

LOGAN

Sorry about earlier, on the roof. I don't know what came over me.

I stare at his message for a long time. How much courage it must have taken him to write those words, and twice as much again to send them. I sigh, thinking long and hard about my reply.

No problem. It was pretty hot up there—I figured the sun just fried your brain. 😉

Fried your brain? Ugh. I delete what I wrote and type something else.

No problem. It was an honest mistake.

Except that it wasn't—he knew exactly what he was doing. I shake my head and try again.

TAYLOR

No problem

I hit send when nothing better comes to mind for a full minute.

Crawling under the covers, I stare at the ceiling, thinking about this afternoon. The look in Logan's eyes and the sound of his voice when he said my name felt like a siren call, and in the darkness I close my eyes, imagining what it would have felt like to let him kiss me.

Abruptly I sit up, throwing off my blankets in an effort to cool my flaming body. I shouldn't think about kissing Logan. I shouldn't *want* to think about kissing Logan. I drop my face in my hands, groaning.

It's true that I've always been massively goal-driven, but my career has become an all-too-convenient reason for avoiding attachments and relationships of any kind, when the real reason is far more painful to acknowledge.

I hate when my sister is right.

But Rachel doesn't get to decide how long it takes me to heal or how I manage to cope with the loss of our parents, anymore than I got to dictate how she handled her own grief. Logan has—with his blasted charismatic tenacity—managed to worm his way into my life, but I'm not going to let him break the barriers of my heart.

I grab my phone from the nightstand and type another text to Logan.

TAYLOR

The picnic was fantastic, and the scarf is
beautiful. I love it. I'm so glad we're friends!

Is it too much, tacking that on to the end? I mean, he
obviously got the message this afternoon when I deflected his
almost-kiss. I groan again, falling back onto my pillows.

My sister's words come back to me, from the night she
helped me with the muslin. *"He's going to hope, and hope is
hard to kill."*

Well hard or not, it's going to have to die. I hit send before I
overthink it too much, then silence my phone and go to sleep.

———

Vince's fitting the next day is similar to the fitting for the Met
Gala, with most of the team dancing around the dais. Logan
was notably absent, however, and this time Vince's assistant
stood nearby taking notes. Paul snaps a photo of my face when
Vince isn't looking, but assures me he won't be posting it
without his permission.

Two days later the fabric for my dress arrives. I'm home
when I get the notification, but I had the delivery sent to the
studio. Grabbing the muslin and my purse, I leave the
apartment and head to the subway.

Sitting on the train, I think about Logan. We haven't talked
much since the picnic, and I haven't seen him at all. I'm
surprised how much I miss him, and I consider texting him. I
worry that it would be weird, that I should just give him some
space, but in the end I decide to message him. He's still my
friend; we just need to get over this awkward little blip in our
friendship. When I get off the train, I send him a quick text.

The fabric for my dress arrived!! 🤍

By the time I get to the studio, he still hasn't replied. Disappointed, I pocket my phone and head up the stairs.

The box is waiting for me on my table, and as I set my things down Amelia comes around the corner.

"I was surprised to receive a delivery for you, Miss O'Neill," she says, a hint of disapproval in her voice.

"Is that not allowed?" I ask, worried I may have overstepped. "It's fabric for a personal project, but it's quite expensive, and I was worried about having it delivered to my apartment in case I wasn't home. I paid for it myself."

She says nothing, which I take to mean I'm not in trouble, but neither does she move. I look around for something to open the box with, but the only thing I see are fabric shears, and I'm not ready to die just yet. Pulling out my keys, I stab one into the taped center seam and drag it across the top of the long, skinny box.

I feel awkward opening it with Amelia standing there, but since she makes no move to leave, I try to ignore her. Lifting the flaps, I pull out the packing slip and then a large, plastic-wrapped roll of fabric. A bubble of excitement bursts inside me, and I set it down carefully on the table.

Amelia steps forward and picks up the piece of paper, reading it. "Silk velvet," she says, her finely-lined eyebrows lifting slightly.

"Yes, it's for a dress."

She turns slightly to look at me, her expression unchanged. I flush.

"A dress? Mr. Milton has no need for a dress."

"No, of course not. The dress is for me—I've designed it for myself."

Amelia sets the paper down and turns as if to leave. "As long as you remember that you are Mr. Milton's *personal* designer, and are not to design for anyone else," she says, before heading toward her office.

I stare after her. Surely she doesn't consider my making a dress for myself to be designing for someone else? I make a mental note to check over my contract later, but for now, I turn back to the roll of fabric on the table.

Silk velvet is delicate, and since I don't want the oils from my skin to damage the fabric, I wash my hands and don white cotton gloves before handling the roll. I pull off the plastic, admiring the richness of the color and the fineness of the nap.

Suddenly my phone pings, and the most irrational thought —*it's Logan!*—streaks across my mind. I pull off the gloves and lay them carefully on the table as I reach for my phone.

It *is* Logan. And I can't deny how relieved and glad I feel.

LOGAN

That's great! So we're still on for the wedding?

His question surprises me. Why wouldn't we still be going to the wedding together?

An uncomfortable memory surfaces, of how I handled things at the picnic. Not to mention the late night text I sent. I sigh, guilt twisting inside me. I guess I have some damage control to do.

TAYLOR

Of course we're still on for the wedding! I'm sorry if you thought otherwise. I'm excited to go with you, and excited to show you my dress. ☺

I hit send before thinking my response through, and immediately regret it. *I'm excited to go with you?* Why did I say that! I groan, seeing my sister's disappointed face in my mind.

I'm about to put my phone down and start cutting out the fabric, when another text from Logan comes through.

LOGAN

I can't wait to see it. And can't wait to see you.

I stare at the screen, my heart sinking. So much for trying to kill his hope.

Chapter 25

Between designing Vince's Fashion Week ensembles, I work on my dress whenever I can. I cut out all the fabric at the studio, but Amelia's presence makes me so nervous I decide to assemble it at home in my apartment. Things with Logan are still a little strained, but they get better every day, and things have been mostly normal between us for the last two weeks.

Mostly.

I finish my dress the night before Lynette's wedding. Sliding it on, I take a photo using the full-length mirror in my bedroom and send it to my sister.

> RACHEL
> WOW!! 😄😄 Taylor, you look amazing!! 🔥
> Well done!!

I grin, typing a response with my thumbs.

> TAYLOR
> Thanks

RACHEL

What shoes are you going to wear with it?

TAYLOR

I have some strappy black heels from
Nordstrom I was planning to wear

RACHEL

Perfect

The next day I wake up early, too excited to sleep in. I tell myself (quite firmly) that all of my excitement is for the dress, and the chance I have to finally wear it. It's by far some of my best work, and I'm already planning to have some professional photos taken so I can add it to my portfolio. But there's a tiny little voice inside drawing hearts around the name Logan in my mind, and she's getting hard to ignore.

I'm sliding the last bit of color across my lips that evening when I hear Logan's knock on the door. Excitement zips through me, and I have to stop myself from running my hands down the front of my dress. Switching off the bathroom light, I head to the door to open it.

I'm not surprised to see Logan in a suit—I knew the wedding was a black tie affair, after all—but I *am* surprised at the bouquet of roses in his hands.

"Wow, Taylor, you look..." His eyes are wide, his look one of awe. "Wow."

I smile, warmth spreading through every inch of me. "Thanks."

"So this is the dress?" He steps back and I give him a little twirl, a grin plastered across my face.

"This is it," I say.

His eyes travel up and down, taking in not only the rich, bordeaux-colored fabric, but the delicate, butter-yellow ruffles on the sleeves and hemline. A large white belt cinches my waist, and his eyes pause, his look calculating.

"Hmm," he says, and I can practically hear his mind working. "Based on what I remember from the show, I'd say you took your inspiration from a Crimson Pride orchid."

My smile widens. "That's exactly what I did. Do you think I succeeded?"

I turn again, this time more slowly, deliberately, mindful of how the dress accents my curves. When I stop again, facing him, there are two bright spots of red on each of his cheeks. He clears his throat.

"It's amazing," he says, somewhat dazed. His look gives me an unexplainable thrill. Then, as if suddenly remembering the flowers in his hand, he thrusts them towards me. "These are for you. I thought it would be fitting, since your dress was inspired by the flower show we attended. Orchids aren't really bouquet flowers, so I got these instead."

I take them from his hand and bury my nose in the blossoms. "Thank you," I say. "Let me put them in some water and then we can go."

I take the flowers into the kitchen and pull a vase from under the sink. I feel giddy and excited, the first reaction to my self-designed dress a huge success. Turning on the faucet, I fill the vase with water and arrange the roses in it.

I carry the arrangement into the living room, and when I set it on the coffee table I have a sudden idea.

"Give me a minute," I say to Logan as I rush past him into my bedroom. The scarf he made for me has been sitting folded on my dresser since the picnic, but now I pick it up, holding it gently in my hands. Standing in front of the mirror, I carefully arrange it around my neck. The color perfectly matches the ruffles on my dress.

I walk back out to where Logan is waiting. "Alright, now I'm ready."

"Great, I—" His voice abruptly cuts off, and I pause. He has one hand on the door handle, but his body and expression are frozen, staring at me. I thought it would be a nice accessory for the evening, but then I remember the disastrous almost-kiss when he gave me the scarf, and heat fills my cheeks.

"I'm sorry, I can take it off," I say. "I just thought it would look nice, you know? Since it matches so well." I take a step backwards, about to turn.

But Logan finally thaws. "No, don't take it off," he says, reaching out to me. I look down at his outstretched hand, remembering the library, and he drops his arm.

"Please, keep it on," he says.

His smile is soft; not wide enough to accent the cleft in his chin, but I find myself thinking about it anyway.

"Okay, if you're sure," I say, watching him.

"I'm sure." His grin widens, and his dimple peeks out at me. Holding out his elbow, he lifts one eyebrow. "Shall we, Miss O'Neill?"

A rush of warmth shivers through me, and I take his arm. "Lead on, Mr. Alexander."

———

The 3 West Club is one of the prime wedding venues in Manhattan, so it's no surprise that Lynette chose it for hers. I thought it would feel strange riding the subway in such formal clothes, but the way Logan keeps looking at me leaves very little room for any other thought. I feel tongue-tied sitting next to him, which is a strange experience. I've always enjoyed how easy he is to talk to.

At last we arrive at the hotel and make our way inside. Logan holds open every door for me, until we get to the room where the ceremony will be held. Two spectacular chandeliers hang from the ceiling, reflected in the mirrors lining the walls. Floor-to-ceiling windows framed with rich, golden drapes line the length of one wall, and on either end of the long, narrow room are two beautiful fireplaces. Flowers and candles are everywhere.

"This is beautiful," I say.

"It is," Logan replies, but he's looking at me when he says it. I try not to blush.

"I haven't been to a wedding in a long time—not since my sister got married," I say.

"Me neither."

I gasp in mock surprise. "You were at my sister's wedding?" I tease, looking at him with wide eyes.

He laughs and bumps my shoulder, just as the middle-aged mom from his knitting club comes up the aisle.

"Hey Logan, can we sit with you guys?" she asks.

"Oh, hi Sarah. Of course," Logan says.

We move over to make room for Sarah and her husband, whom she introduces to us.

"Have you seen any of the others?" she asks.

"Not yet," Logan says. "But I'm sure—"

I tap his arm, and when he turns back to me I point over his shoulder. Just entering the room are Madge and Fumie, the former woman's hair now a vivid shade of pink.

"I like that better than the blue," I say, amused.

The two of them claim a couple of seats near the back, which is probably for the best. Logan catches Fumie's eye and offers her a small wave. She nudges Madge and the both of them wave wildly at us.

"Not subtle at all, those two," I chuckle. "Do you think they'll behave themselves?"

"They better," Logan mutters, "or Lynette will have their heads."

"I love your scarf, Taylor," Sarah says. "Do you mind if I...?" Her voice trails off.

"No, not at all."

She picks up the trailing end of the scarf to inspect the stitches. "It's such detailed handiwork," she says. Looking up at Logan she asks, "Is this what you've been working on?"

I look to Logan, and find he's been watching me with that same soft smile on his face he wore at my apartment. I blush. "Logan?" I say.

He blinks and looks to Sarah. "What? Oh, yes."

She gives him an amused smile. "We didn't realize it was for Taylor," she says, then gives me a knowing look. "Cashmere?" she asks him.

"It's a silk blend. Custom dyed from Expression Fiber Arts."

"And didn't you come up with the design yourself?"

He grins. "I did, yes."

My eyebrows shoot up. "You designed the pattern yourself?"

He nods, his smile growing.

I pick up the loop of scarf that hangs below my collarbone, looking at it with new eyes. Slowly I look back at his face.

"Do you know what this means, Logan?" I ask, not breaking my gaze. "We're both designers."

Surprise flits across his face, followed by a slow, steady smile. It lights up his face, drawing out his dimple and giving a glimpse of his teeth.

My pulse skyrockets in response.

Sarah's voice breaks into my thoughts. "Well, it's beautiful, and it looks lovely on you, Taylor," she says. She gives me a warm smile, then flashes it at Logan as well.

"Thanks. I like it, too," I say, reaching up and gently fingering the edge.

In spite of my electric awareness of Logan beside me the entire time, the wedding is lovely. The bride wears a tasteful pantsuit of dove gray; her groom in a tailored suit of a slightly darker shade. When the officiator pronounces them man and wife and their lips finally meet, a shrill whistle pierces the room. I turn to see Madge standing in the back, the pinkie fingers of each hand stuck between her lips. The guests laugh and cheer for the new couple, and she whistles again. Fumie smacks her arm.

Slowly the guests spill out of the room and into an adjacent one for the reception. Logan leads us to our assigned table, where The Grannies™ and Jonathan are already seated.

"Looks like Lynette kept the club together," Jonathan says as he gets to his feet, shaking Logan's hand. "Hello again, Taylor."

"Hi Jonathan," I say, taking the seat Logan pulls out for me. Madge and Fumie give each other a look. "We didn't see you earlier."

"I was sitting near the front, with Cordelia. We arrived quite early."

"I'm glad Cordelia could make it," Logan says. "Where is she?"

"Getting a drink," Fumie cuts in. "We told her to send Jonathan but she insisted on going herself."

"I don't blame her," Madge says, taking a sip from her glass. "Have you seen the young man working the bar?"

She makes a *mmm*ing sound, as if she were eating something especially delicious, causing the rest of us to laugh. Fumie just rolls her eyes.

Sarah and her husband soon join us, and a few minutes later Cordelia shuffles over, holding a glass of white wine in her hand.

"That is a lovely scarf, Taylor," Cordelia says, coming to stand beside me. Logan jumps up and pulls her chair out for her. She gives him an airy smile.

"Thank you," I say.

"It's the one Logan's been working on," Sarah pipes up, and the friends all share looks around the table. I blush.

"I wondered if it was. It's exquisite," Cordelia says. She pats my hand. "And it goes so well with your dress. Where did you get it?"

"It's my own creation," I say modestly.

"That's right, you're a designer," Jonathan says. "So it's an original?"

I nod, and exclamations ripple around the table. I try to keep my smile unaffected, feeling self-conscious, but Logan is beaming beside me.

"It's stunning," Jonathan says when the murmurs die down. "Who are you designing for?"

"A private label," I say smoothly. "But this one was just for me."

"I like the ruffles," Madge says from across the table.

"You have some serious talent," Sarah adds.

Murmurs of agreement chorus her words, and Logan gives me a smug look, leaning closer.

"Told you," he murmurs, quiet enough only I can hear.

"You're all so kind," I say. "Thank you. It was fun to make, for sure."

The conversation turns to other topics, and soon dinner is served. Logan and I have the salmon, which is delicious, but a few of the group requested the chicken plate, including Madge. She keeps sticking her fork on Fumie's plate to nab pieces of her dinner, while Fumie swats at her arm and swears at her in Japanese. At least, it sounds like she's swearing.

After dinner and the toasts, the cake is cut and the dancing begins. The light streaming in from the outside windows has been gradually fading, and in the soft glow of sunset dozens of candles are lit around the room. When Logan stands up, a burst of anticipation explodes in my belly and I have to swallow it back, trying to ignore the swooping sensation inside. But he asks Cordelia to join him, and in the fizzle of disappointment that follows I turn to Jonathan.

"Care to dance?" I ask.

He looks surprised for a moment, then a sly smile lights up his face. "You're not really my type, Taylor."

I chuckle. "Fair enough," I say, grinning. But Fumie *tsks* at him.

"Get out there Jonathan, before I come over there and make you."

He laughs and holds up his hands in surrender before getting to his feet. "Alright, alright. Come on Taylor, let's dance."

We find a spot on the dance floor and take our positions. "How're things with Logan?" he asks as we turn in a slow circle.

"What do you mean?"

He gives me a wry look. "You remember what I told you when you came to knitting club, don't you?" I nod, and he continues. "If you haven't noticed the way he's been looking at you all night, you must be blind."

"What do you mean?" I say again, although I know *exactly* what he means. Logan has been wearing that soft smile ever since he picked me up, and every time I glance at him he's watching me. Just thinking about it causes the now-familiar fluttering to fill my belly again.

Jonathan lets out an exasperated chuckle. "Taylor, you seem like a really nice person. Don't string him along, okay? If you're not interested, you need to tell the guy before he gets his heart broken."

"He's known all along," I say, a bite of defensiveness in my voice. "We're just friends."

He shakes his head. "You are so much more than that to him, Taylor. You have to see that."

We go back to the table after the dance, and Logan and Jonathan do their duty by the old ladies. They take each of them in turn onto the dance floor, and I watch them all, laughing and clapping at some of their antics. Madge insists on dancing the tango when Logan asks her to join him on the floor, and Logan, never one to do things halfway, even sneaks a flower from a nearby arrangement to clutch between his teeth.

The night feels magical.

After what seems like an eternity, Logan turns to face me. I've been half afraid that he would ask me to dance, but more afraid that he wouldn't. Have I pushed him so far away as that? But his eyes are alight, his expression open as he holds out his hand.

"Shall we?" he asks, nodding his head at the dancing couples.

I glance at his open palm, and a wicked grin slides across my face. I shrug, pretending indifference.

"I haven't got your knife, sorry."

It takes him half a second before he bursts out laughing, and then I join him. The others look at us in confusion.

"Sorry guys," Logan says. "Inside joke."

I take his hand and we head toward the cluster of dancers in the middle of the floor. Turning to face me, he glances down at our joined hands.

"I'm glad you didn't have a knife," he says conversationally, "or this could have been awkward."

I laugh quietly, but as he sets his other hand at my waist, my heart jumps into my throat, choking the sound into silence. His fingers are soft and warm around my right hand, and as I place my left hand on his shoulder my heart hiccups.

For a minute or two, we don't say anything—just turn and sway with the music, watching the other dancers and the guests still seated at the surrounding tables.

"They look really happy," I say, noticing Lynette and her doctor floating around the dance floor.

"They do," Logan says, following my line of sight. "I just hope he can keep up with her."

"Can anyone?" I ask, and I hear his low chuckle in response. The sound spills into my heart like warm honey.

We lapse into comfortable silence, letting the music wrap around us as we dance. Slowly, as if waiting to see how I'll react, Logan's hand slides to my lower back and he pulls me closer. My heart rate spikes, but I don't pull away.

"Thanks for coming with me tonight," he says softly.

"Thanks for inviting me," I say, my voice matching his.

"You know, I wasn't sure you'd actually say yes when I asked," he says. "And then, after the picnic, I wasn't sure if you still wanted to come. But I'm glad you did."

I simply nod, afraid of what I might say if I open my mouth.

Logan bends his head down, his lips brushing my ear. "I'm not sure I told you before," he says, "but you look amazing tonight."

I shiver involuntarily, cursing my careening heart.

"Like an orchid," he murmurs, "only more beautiful."

For a moment, I wonder what it would feel like to surrender to this. To close my eyes and relax into his arms. I rest my head against his shoulder, feeling a pull inside I'm so tired of fighting.

Gently he rests his head against mine. "I never want this night to end," he breathes, so quietly I wonder if he even meant for me to hear him.

"Neither do I," I say, equally as quiet.

And then, realizing what I just said, I freeze.

I'm in love with Logan.

The icy grip of panic claws its way up my throat, stealing my breath and nearly choking me. I push against him suddenly, breaking free from his embrace. "I need a drink," I say frantically, looking down at my feet, around at the tables, back toward the entrance—anywhere but at him.

"Sure, I'll get you some water," he says, surprise coloring his words.

"No, I need a *drink*."

Before he can respond, I'm rushing toward the bar, desperate to escape him and the terrifying feelings I've tried to ignore.

"Bourbon," I tell the man standing on the other side of the table. He picks up a glass and pours a small amount of amber liquid into it before handing it to me. Logan reaches my side just as I toss my head back and down the drink in two gulps. Fire burns down my throat, making me cough.

"Taylor," Logan says, and I can't stop myself from looking at him this time. He's not smiling, and his eyes are intent on my face.

"I have to go," I gasp, setting the glass down and moving past him again.

"Taylor, wait," he says, reaching for my arm, but I slide through his grip and keep walking.

"What just happened?" he calls from behind me, obviously trying to catch up.

"I had a drink," I say, without turning or stopping. "And now I'm going home."

I can see his knitting club clustered around the table ahead of us, chatting with each other, oblivious to our approach.

"That's not what I meant," he says.

I snatch up my purse and my phone from the table, startling Fumie into exclaiming something in Japanese. I turn around to walk back to the entrance and collide with Logan.

His arms shoot out to steady me, and I wobble for a moment before finding my feet. My arms are hot beneath his hands, and when he lets go of me he takes all the heat with him.

"Are you really going home?" he asks, his voice low. Concerned.

I nod, not trusting my own voice. Suddenly I want to cry,

and the embarrassment and shame I feel courses hot through my veins. The final notes of the song linger softly in the air.

"Then I'll come with you."

"No!" I practically shout the word, and in the lull between songs it sounds even louder than I intended. Several guests turn to stare at us. Madge *tsks* reprovingly behind me.

"No," I say, more quietly this time. "You stay here. I'll be fine." Without waiting to hear his response, I hurry away, leaving my neighbor—and my heart—behind me.

Chapter 26

I cry myself to sleep that night. Rachel texts me the next morning to ask how the wedding was, but I don't respond. I rot in bed until nearly noon, and when I finally claw my way out from under the covers I give my heart a stern talking to.

I never meant for you to get involved, you know.

It throbs in remorse.

People we love don't stick around, I tell it sternly, thinking of my parents. *They always leave us, one way or another, ripping you to shreds in the process. Is that what you want? To be torn to pieces and then desiccated when he leaves?*

My heart pushes against the words, pulling up an image of my sister as evidence to the contrary. I clench my jaw, refusing to yield.

This is why we keep to ourselves. This is why we focus on our work. Loving someone brings nothing but pain and misery, which is nothing but a terrible distraction from our dreams.

My heart cracks open a little more, bleeding tears down my face.

I head to my tiny bathroom and splash water on my swollen

eyes. I brush my teeth and change into some comfy clothes. My bedroom is a mess, and truth be told, so is my whole apartment. I'd been so focused on finishing my dress I neglected nearly everything else for days.

The culprit for my apartment's state of disarray is lying at an angle across the foot of my bed, where I tossed it last night. I pick it up, rubbing my fingers gently over the soft crimson fabric. Swirls of memory fly through my mind, like petals caught in a whirlwind. Card games with Logan. Dinners on the roof. Late night texts. Laughing over memes. Learning how to knit. The flower show, the picnic, the dance...

I sigh, grabbing a hanger from the closet and slipping the dress onto it. I pull out a plastic garment bag, cover the dress, and shove the whole thing into the back of my closet. I try to do the same with the memories that keep surfacing, pushing them into the far recesses of my mind and reminding myself of all the reasons I didn't want to get involved with my neighbor.

My heart thumps painfully in my chest at the lecture.

Heartache can be a terrible thing to endure, but it can also act as fantastic fuel. I spend the rest of the day scrubbing my apartment, blasting my music as loud as I can tolerate and cleaning every inch of space I own. Rachel texts me a few times, but I give her the excuse that I'm not feeling well today and she finally leaves me alone. Logan hasn't texted me, but at one point I think I hear someone knocking on my door. I'm too afraid to find out if it's him, so I ignore it, turning up my music a little more in case he decides to knock again.

———

LOGAN
Hey, can we talk?

It's the first text from Logan since the wedding, three days ago. I stare at the words, not knowing what I can say that won't hurt him, so instead of replying I put my phone down and get back to my design work.

A few hours later he knocks on my door. I know I can't hide from him forever, so I sigh and get up from my drafting table. I may as well get this over with.

I open the door just as Logan is about to knock again. "Oh," he says, letting his arm drop. "I didn't think you'd open the door."

"That's the funny thing about knocking on someone's door," I say. "They usually answer it." I cringe inside at my caustic tone.

"Except that this is the first time you've answered your door in the last three days."

I shrug, but say nothing. He stares at me, and the longer he stares the more pained his expression becomes. His look makes me wince inside, but it has to be this way.

I keep my expression smooth, looking calmly back at him. "Did you need something?" I prompt, when he still doesn't say anything.

"Are we okay, Taylor?" he asks, looking and sounding for all the world like he's about to cry. A tiny part of me wants to rush forward and throw my arms around him, but I beat her back with every ounce of resolve I can muster.

"We? There is no *we*, Logan."

"You know what I mean."

"Actually, I don't."

His brow lowers just a fraction. "You ran off in the middle of the wedding reception, you ignore my calls, you hardly answer my texts, and I'm starting to wonder if you're climbing down the fire escape to avoid going in and out your front door, just so you don't risk running into me."

(I haven't been. But that's not a bad idea.)

I sigh. "Is there a question in there somewhere?"

"What happened, Taylor?"

"Nothing."

"Something happened. At the reception."

"I had a drink," I say lightly, folding my arms across my chest to hide their trembling.

He narrows his eyes. "Before that."

I sigh in exasperation, dropping my arms. "You tell me then, Logan. What happened?"

The hardened look in his eyes softens. "We danced. I told you you were beautiful. And I said I never wanted the night to end."

He pauses, and I know he's waiting for me to tell him what I said after that. But I press my lips together, determined to remain silent.

"And then you—"

"Went and got a drink. And went home."

The hurt in his eyes nearly unravels me and I look away, forcing my lip not to tremble.

"What's wrong, Taylor? What did I do?"

"Nothing. I've just been busy."

"Busy?"

"Yep. Fashion Week is in less than a month, you know."

"I know, but—"

"I just don't think we should be hanging out as much."

"You don't think..." His face suddenly crumbles. "Are you breaking up with me?"

I force myself to laugh, when all I really want to do is cry. "Breaking up? Logan, we're not dating. We never were. There is no relationship to break up *from*."

He opens his mouth, hurt and confusion warring for dominance in his eyes. "But I thought—"

"Look, I've got to go."

"Taylor—"

"See ya, Logan."

And I close the door.

I stand there for a moment, trying to ignore the gaping hole that's bleeding inside me, trying to ignore the lump in my throat that threatens to choke the breath out of me. *It's better this way,* I try to convince myself. *Better to suffer the pain now than the infinitely worse pain if he were to leave. Besides,* I justify, *relationships are just a distraction, and I can't afford any more distractions. Not right now. Not when I'm so close.*

I don't hear any movement on the other side of the door—no footsteps walking across the landing, no doors opening or shutting. Thinking about Logan standing just on the other side, remembering the last look on his face...

I turn away and stumble to the couch, trying to hold in the tears as my heart rips apart.

Chapter 27

The next morning I pack up and head to my sister's house. The thought of running into Logan on the stairs or at the coffee shop or even at the studio nearly undoes me. I need some space, before I do something really stupid, like tell him that I love him and I was wrong about everything.

Rachel lets me lay on her bed and cry as long as I need. She strokes my hair and listens to me wail, and doesn't once say *I told you so*. When the tears finally dry up, she sighs.

"I'm so sorry, T. I wish I could take this pain away."

I sit up, wiping my face with the hem of my shirt. She gets the tissue box from across the room and sets it beside me.

"You can stay here as long as you like. Marc can probably help with the commute if you need to go back for work; we'll just have to look at your schedules together."

But I shake my head. "I can take the train. I don't want to put you guys out, not when it's been my stupidity to land me in this mess. But thank you."

That plan only lasts a week, however. The train ride from the nearby town of Dover to Manhattan is over three hours, and that much again on the way back. After three commutes I decide it's time to go home and face the consequences of my actions. Rachel hugs me tight, assuring me I can come back anytime.

But I decide to stay in the city. Fashion Week is fast approaching, and the team and I have several outfits for Vince in various stages of completion. I spend more time at the studio than at my apartment, and thankfully Logan isn't there often. The few times I've seen him at work, we were both busy enough that he didn't come over to say hi. The ache in my chest eases a bit with every passing day, until something inevitably reminds me of my charming, dorky neighbor, and then I have to beat down my traitorous heart all over again. It's exhausting.

Vince's popularity has grown steadily all summer long, and the industry is buzzing to know the name of the new designer responsible for his recent success. He's been hinting online that he'll have something exciting to announce during Fashion Week, so I think my time in the spotlight is soon to arrive. My nerves are strung tighter than a pair of David Bowie's pants, waiting for that to happen.

September arrives on a sweltering, red-hot carpet, with temps well above the eighty-degree average. Vince is attending a few fashion shows in person, but his ensembles are ready to go and he hasn't given me any new deadlines. I was hoping to enjoy my little break by catching a few shows in person myself, but when the second week of the month rolls around, I find myself nursing a head cold.

"Thank goodness for livestream," I mutter to myself, wrapping my hands around a large mug of steaming tea.

I've always loved New York Fashion Week. Watching the up-and-coming designers as well as the old standbys—it's always a thrill to see which fashions and trends have lasted another season, and which new ones step into the spotlight. I've gotten pretty good at identifying which trends will stick around and which will die a glorious death, and I'm anxious to see if any of my latest predictions prove correct. Watching the shows from my living room is a painful reminder of watching the Met Gala with Logan, but I do my best to ignore the memories. I refuse to let my melancholy ruin what could be the most important event in my entire career.

The first two days of Fashion Week do not disappoint. My head and my sketchbook fill with fresh ideas, and I can't wait to start working on some new designs. I turn off the tv on Saturday night after the last show of the day, disappointed that I didn't catch a glimpse of Vince in the audience at any point, because I know he was planning to attend that day. But no matter. By tomorrow morning, my social media feed will be loaded with photos and articles from the day's events, as well as mentions and commentary on notable attendees. Vince Milton is *always* mentioned, and often interviewed, so there's a good chance I'll be able to see which outfit of mine he wore *and* get the press's take on it at the same time.

I crawl into bed feeling drowsy and content, and for the first time in a long while I find myself looking forward to the next day.

If only I'd been able to prepare myself for it.

Chapter 28

My phone rings *far* too early for a Sunday the next morning. I groan, realizing I forgot to silence it before bed. I roll over, reaching for it on my bedside table. The clock on the shelf says 6:41 when I answer the call.

"Hello?" My voice is rough from sleep.

"Taylor? Are you okay?"

Rachel sounds worried, which confuses me. I clear my throat. "Yeah, I'm fine. Just sleeping. Why?"

"Oh. Um..." She hesitates. "You've been sleeping? So you haven't... seen anything?"

Alarm bells go off in my head, and I jerk into a sitting position. "Seen what?"

She sighs. "Vince. It's all over the internet. If I had known—"

"I'll call you back," I say, ending the call and pulling up the browser on my phone. My heart is pounding a mile a minute, my hands shaking as I pull up the fashion headlines. Most of the articles are about the various designers and shows participating in this year's Fashion Week, but as I scroll through them I start to see Vince's name pop up.

Emperor365 Turns Heads (and stomachs) at New York Men's Day

Vince Milton Flunks Fashion Week

The Emperor NEEDS New Clothes After Recent Debacle

"I am the victim" - Milton Breaks Silence About New Designer

I click on the last headline, my stomach rolling as I read.

New York Fashion Week is known for bringing out the best, and worst, in fashion and design. Unfortunately for influencer Vince Milton, his personal designer seems to have fallen into the latter category. "I am the victim," Milton said in an exclusive interview last night, "of the most heinous prank the fashion industry has ever known."

Milton was, of course, referring to the disaster he wore to Spring Studios yesterday, which has earned him severe criticism and mockery from even his most loyal fans. According to Milton, he has been having a hard time keeping his naïve young designer in check. "She's come to me with the most ludicrous ideas," he said. "I've had to rein her in and completely overhaul her designs to make them even somewhat decent. But she's been pressuring me to trust her instincts and let her have full rein, so I decided to give her a chance."

The results were catastrophic. Apparently Milton's designer—one Taylor O'Neill by name—has had virtually no design experience. When asked why he chose to take a gamble on her, Milton said...

I stop reading and scroll down, looking for a photo. There, halfway through the article is a picture of Vince, wearing the most hideous thing I've ever seen. A double-breasted satin jacket, made in a chartreuse Pucci print, with cut-off arms. The puffed sleeves of a mauve dress shirt are visible from his shoulders to his wrists. The shirt is one I recognize—by description, at least. It was one of Vince's ideas for the Tony Awards, but I'd shot it down. I didn't know he'd had Amelia make it, and I have no idea where the jacket came from.

It's not my design—none of it is. All of it looks to be fashion of Vince's own making. His careful threats and secretive hints drift back into my head, and now I know why Amelia and her team of seamstresses have been sewing so much, even when I haven't had designs for them to make. My head is spinning at the revelation. How many other clothing items have they all hidden from me? The only reason he outed me now was to save himself from his current humiliation. He hasn't been keeping me as "his little secret," he's been saving me as his emergency scapegoat.

The reality of what has happened settles slowly, until suddenly my stomach turns and I dash for the bathroom. I heave into the toilet, whether from despair or the virus I've been fighting for a week, I don't know. All I know is that I'm finished.

I'm finished before I've even begun.

———

I spend the rest of the day curled up in bed, alternately crying and screaming into my pillow. I thought, when I took the job with Vince, that all my dreams were about to come true. This was supposed to be it; my big break. Instead, the whole situation has turned into something from my worst nightmares.

Logan and Rachel call and text me all day long, but I ignore them both. I know I told my sister this morning I would call her back, but I can't. I wasn't expecting this. I know if I talk to her, she'll rant and rave about how awful Vince is, and tell me that I'm brilliant and too good for him anyway, but nothing will change. Nothing will happen. My name will still be smeared with mud, and all my hopes of ever hitting the red carpet will be buried in the mud with it.

And if I talk to Logan? Well. I haven't been willing to do much of *that* in the last month. I don't even want to know what he would say to me.

But the next afternoon, Logan starts pounding on the door. "Taylor?" he calls. "Taylor, please. Talk to me. I'm worried about you. Are you okay? Taylor? Taylor?" He continues yelling and knocking for several minutes, but at last he leaves. I'm glad, because all the pounding was making my headache even worse.

About twenty minutes later there's another knock on the door. I ignore it, but when the knock comes again, followed by an unfamiliar voice hollering "NYPD. Is anyone home?" I scramble out of bed. Am I being arrested? Did Vince's lies contain something illegal that would send them to my door?

I undo the lock and open the door slightly. I'm still in my

pjs, which are rumpled and damp from sweat and tears. "Yes?" I say, my voice a croak.

"Hello ma'am, I'm Officer White. Are you Taylor O'Neill?"

"Yes," I say again. The door to Logan's apartment opens, and the officer turns.

"Taylor," Logan says, his voice relieved. He looks at the police officer. "I'm the one that called in for the welfare check."

The officer nods. "Ma'am," he says, facing me again, "we just wanted to check in with you and make sure everything is all right. Are you hurt or injured?"

"No," I say, shaking my head.

"Do you mind if I ask you a few questions?"

I force myself not to look at Logan. "Go ahead."

"Can you tell me your full name?"

"Taylor O'Neill."

"Do you know where you are?"

"My apartment in Brooklyn."

"Can you tell me the date?"

"Um..." My head is fuzzy from crying, and I have to think. "September tenth."

He nods. "Do you feel like hurting yourself or anyone else?"

For a fleeting moment, I think about strangling Vince. But I shake my head.

"No. I've been upset by some news, but I don't want anyone to get hurt. I'm okay."

I am most certainly *not* okay, but for his intents and purposes, I am. He nods at me, then at Logan. "All right then. If anything changes or you need any help, just let us know."

"Thank you, officer," Logan calls as the man starts back

down the stairs. He lifts a hand in acknowledgement and continues on his way.

I stand there, looking at Logan's feet because I can't bring myself to look at his face. "You called the police?"

"I didn't have your sister's number, and I was worried about you. You wouldn't answer your phone or the door, and I thought..." He blows out his breath, running a hand up through his hair. "I just wanted to make sure you were okay."

I nod, but I can feel the tears start to flow, so I take a step back and move to shut the door. In two quick steps he pushes it open and wraps his arms around me. "I'm so sorry, Taylor," he says. "This is all my fault."

I'm so surprised at his sudden embrace I forget that I should be pushing him away. Instead, I bury my face in his chest and sob, letting him hold me. He doesn't say anything else, and neither do I—we just stand there in the doorway together, mourning. After several minutes my sobs slow down and I pull away. He lets me go and I wipe at my eyes, pulling up the hem of my tshirt to wipe my dripping nose. Logan puts his hands gently on my shoulders and ducks his head to look me in the eyes.

"I'm going to fix this, Taylor. He's a liar, and I won't let him do this to you."

I shake my head, the tears starting again, and he wraps me in his arms once more. This time I put my arms around him, too; drawing on his strength, trying to force myself to believe that something, anything, can be done to fix this. But I don't believe him. Nothing can fix this.

Nothing.

Chapter 29

R achel shows up a few hours later, also concerned about me. She has an overnight bag and says she can stay as long as I need—Marc took some emergency PTO and she insists. She makes me chicken soup and cleans up all the dirty dishes I've ignored since getting sick, just like when we were kids. I can't bring myself to watch any more of Fashion Week, and although I'm morbidly curious about what other lies Vince has spread about me, Rachel threatens to take away my phone if I go reading anything else.

The cherry on top of the fallout with Vince comes the day after my sister arrives. Glancing through my email I find a termination notice from him, sent the day the news articles were published. And actually, it's not even *from* Vince, but from his assistant. My sister hears my hysteric cries and races into my bedroom, worried that I've had another meltdown, but I'm laughing so hard I can't even breathe. By the time I manage to convey what has happened, the ironic hilarity of the situation has worn off enough that my laughs turn to sobs, and I melt into a puddle on the floor.

That evening, I send a text to Logan.

> TAYLOR
>
> Hey

He responds almost immediately.

> LOGAN
>
> Hey. How are you feeling?

> TAYLOR
>
> About as good as you'd expect

> LOGAN
>
> That bad, huh?

> TAYLOR
>
> Worse

> LOGAN

I stare at the screen for a long time before taking a deep breath.

> TAYLOR
>
> I owe you the world's biggest apology

> LOGAN
>
> It's ok. I've been talking to your sister. I think I understand why you did what you did.

I frown. He's been talking to Rachel? I wrack my brain. When the police showed up for the welfare check, he told me he didn't have her number, so it has to have been since she's been here with me. Did she sneak over to talk to him when I was sleeping sometime? Did they finally exchange numbers? Have they been texting each other behind my back? I shake my head, dislodging the questions and letting them drift away unanswered. It doesn't matter, I guess. I look back down at my phone.

> TAYLOR
>
> I was a jerk

> LOGAN
>
> Don't. Please. Hurt people, hurt people. I get it. We can chat in a few days, when you're feeling better, k?

I swallow past the lump in my throat, my vision going blurry.

> TAYLOR
>
> Okay. Thanks, Logan.

He sends a heart emoji in response, and I look at it for a long time, marveling that after everything I've said, everything I've done, he might just forgive me.

———

On Wednesday I finally drag myself back into the land of the living and start thinking about my future. I'm not too proud to go crawling back to Totsworth (if they'll even have me), but I don't think I'm ready to do that just yet. I need to make sure I won't burst into tears if anyone asks what I've been up to for the last six months. Not that they will—I'm sure they've all seen the articles by now, and I can practically see Marjorie and Jason's gloating faces in my mind.

Ugh. Maybe Greg will let me work remotely.

The next couple days are easier. I'm finally over my cold, and Rachel and I spend some time watching some of our favorite old movies together. She even manages to convince me to do some living room yoga, even though there's not enough room for both of us. I'll admit, it definitely helps to move my body and clear my head, but it's going to take a lot more yoga to get over this catastrophe.

Just as I'm getting out of the shower on Friday morning, my phone pings with an email notification. I pull on my robe and reach for my phone, my stomach filled with dread. Is it another news article? More hate mail from Vince Milton's fans?

But it's neither of those things. It's an email from the contact form attached to my online portfolio, and I frown, opening it.

Dear Ms. O'Neill,

Please forgive my forwardness, but I have just seen the recent video posted on Emperor365's Instagram account. I am so sorry you've been the victim of his arrogant games, and I want to express my support for you in your pursuit of a career in fashion. The work you've done for Milton is stunning, and after a perusal of your online portfolio, I am even more impressed. If you would ever consider joining us at Durante & Delphine, we would be honored to have you.

Sincerely,
Katherine Howald

Confused, I read the email again. I recognize the name of the sender—she's one of the Vice Presidents at Durante & Delphine and one of the biggest names in fashion. But why is she writing to me? And what video is she talking about?

Hesitant, I pull up Vince's Instagram account. The featured video doesn't show Vince, but... Logan?

"Hi everyone. In case you couldn't tell, I'm not Vince Milton," Logan says, looking at the camera. "My name is Logan Alexander, and I'm Emporer365's I.T. guy. Or was, I should say, since I resigned after the stunt he pulled a few days ago."

My jaw drops. How did Logan get away with this?

"Everything Vince Milton has said about his designer, Taylor O'Neill, is a lie. And I should know, because I'm the one who introduced him to her in the first place. She's a genius, and it has been *her* keeping *him* in check for the last several months. That outfit he wore to Spring Studios? Not Taylor's design. That was 100% Vince, and the whole reason it was so hideous."

I watch, stunned, as Logan goes through and methodically debunks everything Vince has said about me that was untrue. Some of it I hadn't heard, and my stomach turns thinking about what a slimeball he is. The video cuts to screenshots of emails and text messages supporting Logan's claims. How did he get access to those? That was private correspondence between me and Vince. And isn't Logan under a gag order as well?

"As you can see," Logan says, his face on the camera again, "Vince Milton is *not* the victim here. Taylor O'Neill is. She doesn't deserve the censure and ridicule she's received because of the actions of her previous employer. Taylor O'Neill is..." His face flushes. "Taylor is amazing. Seriously, she's amazing. She's funny, and smart, and kind, and the most brilliant designer I've ever known. All the incredible pieces you've seen Vince wearing in the last six months have been her work. All of it. She's going places, and I wouldn't be at all surprised if she's one of the top names in fashion someday."

My throat constricts, and the tears that have been so close

to the surface for days spill down my cheeks. But these are happy tears, and I wipe them away quickly, not wanting to miss the end of the video.

Logan puts my online portfolio web address and business email on the screen, encouraging viewers to check out my designs and to stop following Vince Milton. "He doesn't deserve any more of your accolades," he tells the camera. "Taylor does."

The video ends, and I drop my phone in my lap, reaching up to wipe my eyes again. I start laughing, but the tears keep coming.

"Taylor? Are you ok?"

Rachel peeks her head into my room, and, seeing me crying, comes inside. "Oh T," she says. "Are you—"

"Have you seen this?" I ask, picking up my phone and thrusting it at her.

"Seen what?"

I tap the screen and hand it to her, watching her face as she watches the video, reliving all the emotions I felt just a moment ago.

"But how did he...?"

"I don't know," I say, shaking my head. "But I'm going to find out."

I rush to get dressed, not caring that my makeup isn't on and my hair is still a wet, bedraggled mess. I snatch up my phone and head for the landing, knocking briskly on Logan's door.

He opens it after just a few moments. "Taylor! How are—"

"How did you do this?" I say, holding up my phone and showing him the screen with his own face staring back at him. He smirks, ducking his head.

"I'm a hacker, remember?" His smile is sheepish. "I had to do *something*."

"You hacked Vince's account?"

"Yeah."

"And his email?"

"And his phone," he sighs.

I stare at him.

"I, uh..." Logan rubs the back of his neck, which has turned red, "also hacked a couple of your accounts. Just to clean up some of the negative comments and posts," he finishes in a rush. "I'm sorry if I overstepped. I just couldn't sit still and see this happen to you."

He hacked my accounts? The information doesn't really register, but I nod anyway. "Thank you for telling me."

"I'm really sorry, Taylor. I should have asked first."

I blink at him. "What? Oh, I'm not upset," I say. "I'm impressed, actually."

"Really?"

"Yeah. I mean, that's pretty big. Hacking into a celebrity's accounts can't be easy."

He grins. "It wasn't. It was fun, though—more complicated than I expected, but definitely worth it."

"Do you think you'll get in trouble? I'm sure you broke some privacy laws or rules or something. Isn't there a gagging clause in your contract?"

Logan shrugs. "Nah, I've been with him too long—I actually sent *him* our first contract. And we never really updated anything legally. I'm not too worried. Vince is probably panicking right now, worried that you might sue him for defamation or something."

I shudder. "That's probably not going to happen. I never want to see that man again in my life."

We stand in silence for a moment, the weight of the last six days slowly dropping from my shoulders. Everything is still a mess, and it's going to take a while to get it all cleaned up, but Logan cleared my name. Logan went out of his way to fix this, the thing I didn't think was possible to fix.

Remorse washes through me, flooding my cheeks with heat. "Logan, I need to apologize. You have been nothing but kind to me, and I've been just awful. I'm so sorry. About everything."

"It's fine."

"No, it's not. I was horrible to you, from the very beginning." My voice cracks, and I clear my throat, trying to swallow my shame. "Do you know why I kept pushing you away?"

He shrugs. "When I was first trying to ask you out, you always made excuses about work. You talked about nothing getting in the way of your career. But after talking with your sister," he rubs his neck again, squinting at me, "I gather that wasn't the only reason."

I nod, grateful that Rachel helped fill him in. "My career has always been the excuse. But the truth is, I've been terrified to love someone again. My dad..." I have to swallow back my tears, "he drank himself to death. So learning you were a recovering alcoholic was a heavy blow."

He nods, his look serious.

"But if I'm being honest, that was just an excuse, too. Because you're not him. You're *nothing* like him. I believe you when you say you're sober. But you have to understand that it wasn't just my dad. After he died," my voice hitches, and I take a steadying breath, "my mom left us. She abandoned us. And that loss hurt, too. Losing both of them? It nearly killed me."

My voice is soft, and I can't look up at him anymore. "You were the best friend I could have asked for, but I kept pushing you away because I was terrified that if I loved you, you would leave me, too."

A sob catches in my throat. "I'm sorry about the picnic," I whisper. "I'm sorry about the wedding reception. And for everything after that, too. It wasn't fair *or* kind of me. Especially when you've been so... so..."

"Annoyingly persistent?" he asks helpfully.

I laugh through my tears. I *love* that he makes me laugh.

"Amazing," I say, wiping my eyes. "You're amazing, Logan." I stretch up on my toes and press a kiss to his cheek.

He grins, then shoves his hands into his pockets. "So, are we ok?"

I shrug, trying to laugh off the bubbly sensation his smile elicits in my gut. "Yeah, we're ok. I mean, I've been a huge jerk, and I'm really, really sorry. But if you'll forgive me, I think we'll be okay. I just wish I could make it up to you."

His look turns calculating. "Hmm. You know, there actually *is* something you could do for me."

"What's that?"

He holds out his hand. Laughing quietly, I put mine into his, and he weaves our fingers together.

"You can let me take you on a date."

This time I laugh in earnest. I pull my hand free and throw my arms around his neck. Startled but pleased, he puts his arms around me as well.

"I've got a better idea," I say, pulling back to look at him.

"Better than a date with you? I don't know, that's a pretty big—"

He doesn't finish because I kiss him. I kiss him for all the wonderful, quirky ways he lets me know he cares. I kiss him for putting up with all my pushback but never giving up on me. I kiss him for all the times he's made me laugh, and all the times he'll make me laugh in the future. I kiss him like my life depends on him, because I realize now that it does.

Somewhere in all the kissing we become tangled up in one another. His arms are around me, holding me close and tight, and I can finally feel the wiry texture of his hair as I thread my fingers through it. His lips press against mine, gentle but earnest, and the heady feeling of falling in love keeps me kissing him over and over again.

I don't know how long we've been standing there on the landing, wrapped up in each other, but eventually he breaks free and rests his forehead against mine. My eyes flutter open as my breathing slows, and he's looking at me in wonder.

"Taylor O'Neill," he says, his voice husky, "if I'd have known you could kiss like that I wouldn't have been so patient."

I laugh quietly, closing my eyes again, reveling in the feeling of his arms around me. I reach for him until my lips meet his, and I fall into his kiss all over again.

"It's about time."

My eyes fly open and I try to pull away, but Logan tightens his grip. Turning my head, I see my sister, leaning against my doorway with her arms folded across her chest, a smug smile on her face.

"Rachel!" My voice comes out high and sharp, my face aflame.

She laughs. "Oh, don't look so surprised, I've been watching since you walked out of the apartment."

I groan and drop my head against Logan's chest. He chuckles and pulls me closer, kissing the top of my head. I hear my sister sigh in contentment.

"Alright, you've had your fun," I say, turning my head to glare at her, "now leave us alone." She laughs, then walks back into my apartment and shuts the door. I sigh, burying my face in Logan's shirt.

"Did you know she was there?" I ask, almost afraid of the answer.

"No," he says, brushing his lips against my temple, then kissing down my cheek and along my jaw, until he presses a kiss to my lips. "I may have heard the door open at some point, but I was a little too preoccupied to pay much attention."

I groan again and he laughs, the rumble in his chest sending shivers of delight coursing through me. I wrap my arms around his neck and tip my head back, looking into his face.

"Logan Alexander, do you love me?" I ask.

His look softens. "You didn't leave me any other choice, Taylor."

"Well, I have a choice," I say. "And I choose *you.*"

Going up on my toes, I press another kiss to his lips and finally step away. His arm reaches out for me and I give him my hand. He looks down at our intertwined fingers and smiles.

"Now, about that date..." he says.

I laugh, letting him pull me into another kiss.

Epilogue

Three years later

The lights are blinding as I peek around the curtain to catch a glimpse of the crowd. I can see Rachel sitting on the right side near the middle of the catwalk. Beside her is my fiancé, Logan. He wanted to help with the tech stuff, but I told him I wanted him to *experience* my first show, not work on it.

I step back into the shadows, closing my eyes as I take a deep, cleansing breath. *This is it,* I think to myself. My phone vibrates in my pocket, and I pull it out quickly, hoping it's not last-minute bad news.

> **LOGAN**
> Don't stress, it's going to be great

I chuckle. He couldn't have seen me, but he knows me well enough to guess that I'd be panicking right about now. His text helps settle my nerves. Before I can type a reply, another message arrives.

> **LOGAN**
> None of your models are wearing a muppet
> suit, so at least you've got that going for you

I laugh. It's just like Logan to make a joke in order to counter my anxiety.

TAYLOR

Don't be so sure. You haven't seen all my designs yet.

I switch my phone to silent and slip it back into my pocket, grinning. *Logan.* Who would have thought I'd ever end up with a handsome, geeky guy who likes growing flowers and knitting socks? Certainly not me. But if it wasn't for him, I wouldn't even be here, living my dream.

One of the show managers rushes past me, glancing briefly in my direction. Suddenly she stops and hurries back. "There you are! Mariah has been looking for you—are you ready?"

I nod and follow her back the way she came. The models are queued up and ready to go, and I offer them smiles and nods as I pass. I stop beside the two screens showing the view from the cameras poised at the end of the catwalk, as *Confident* by Demi Lovato starts playing over the speakers.

"Here we go," I whisper.

The first model heads out as the show begins. On one screen I see the flashing of cameras and the excited looks of the attendees. In the corner of the other screen, I can see Logan's face. It's full of wonder, and my stomach flips in response. I glance down at the ring on my finger.

Once upon a time, I dreamed of seeing my designs on runways and red carpets across the world. From L.A. to New York and Paris to Beijing, I wanted my name to be on the lips of everyone worth knowing. I dreamed of being famous, and having my designs sought after far and wide.

But I've since found a different dream. A much *better*

dream. A dream filled with cozy, hand-knit sweaters and chai lattes on the roof. A dream of Star Wars marathons and arguments over which celebrity wore it best. A dream without any emperors, kings, or celebrities—just me and my guy.

And it's the best dream I ever could have imagined.

THE END

Other books by Shaela Kay

Contemporary romance

Only Ever Friends
Only Ever Christmas

Historical romance

A Heart Made of Indigo
Scoundrel In Disguise
The Rodenburg Girl

Christmas at Edgewood Park
Christmas at Cartwright Manor

To Train a Heart

*If you enjoyed the book, please consider
leaving a review!*

Acknowledgments

"*I can no other answer make, but thanks, and thanks, and ever thanks.*" William Shakespeare said it best, but I will try to add my own humble thanks to his.

To my Heavenly Parents, for blessing me with the time, talents, and means to follow this little dream of mine.

To Clarissa Wilstead for inviting me to participate in a fairy tale anthology back in 2022. From that little novella bloomed this fun story, and I'm so glad it first had a home with the other great authors in *Once Upon a Fairy Tale*.

For the Radioactive Tumbleweeds, who were always ready and willing to listen to my ramblings and hash out story stuff.

Special thanks go to Carrie Jensen and Krista Jensen (no relation), who read early drafts and told me what needed fixing. Amanda Ostler, Kim McCoy, and Jenaca Willans also helped me polish up the final draft. You ladies are the best!

For my bestie Sally Treanor, for everything.

To the love of my life, my husband John. Thanks for believing in me and my dreams even when I didn't. And for my children, who think I'm the best author in the world because they think I'm the best mom in the world. I'm neither, but your faith and belief in me means everything to me. 🩶

And for you, dear readers. Thank you for spending some of your precious time between these pages. You're the reason I put myself through the ~~misery~~ ~~torture~~ *delight* of publishing my stories, instead of letting them stay on my computer forever. I hope you enjoyed it!

About the Author

Shaela Kay was born and raised near Seattle, WA. She studied Theatre and English at Brigham Young University-Idaho, but left her studies in order to be a wife and mother. When she isn't reading or writing, you can find her quilting, crafting, or working as a graphic designer. She and her family live in Washington along the banks of the mighty Columbia River. You can visit her online at www.shaelakay.com

www.ingramcontent.com/pod-product-compliance
Lightning Source LLC
Chambersburg PA
CBHW060913250626
47159CB00008B/2987